I0577958

NOT TOMAHAWK

Sandy Dobson

Copyright © 2024 Sandy Dobson
All rights reserved.

The characters and events portrayed in this book are fictitious. Any similarity to real persons, living or dead, is coincidental and not intended by the author.

No part of this book may be reproduced, or stored in a retrieval system, or transmitted in any form or by any means, electronic, mechanical, photocopying, recording, or otherwise, without express written permission of the publisher.

ISBN-13: 9781763812000

Cover design by: Anze Ban Virant - ABV Atelier Design

For my uncle, a lovely man.

PART 1

Monday 30 May 2022 4.32 pm

I write this sitting in a vast bustling food hall, situated next to Southern Cross train station in Melbourne. My seat is a wobbly metal stool at a bench, hidden behind a pillar. Close by, on my right, is an L-shaped corridor to the toilets, with another way out. If necessary, I can try and run that way.

At the table in front of me sit an extended, excited family group with enormous suitcases. Next to them, a tableful of hi vis wearing tradies give off a relaxed, finished work vibe. Perched on another stool, a guy with an enormous neck tattoo, in a light grey shiny suit, taps away on his laptop. Teenage girls in dark blue school uniforms are being loud at another table. A cute little brown and grey bird hops around snatching crumbs here and there, I hope it can find its way out again.

It's noisy, echoey. Strong smells of coffee and grease. A bit of a sweet smell, ice cream? Food options around me are sushi, salad, pizza, other hot food. Ice cream is tempting me, but for now I'm just making my long black coffee last as long as possible.

High above me is the enormous, curving roof of the station, unpopular with some. To me it's beautiful, like ocean waves from beneath.

Hundreds of people stream past on their way to trains or shops or their homes, half of them wearing masks. Office workers dressed in black, clutching overpriced coffees. Young couples possessively holding hands. An elderly woman grabbing tightly onto the arm of an elderly man, out of fear or maybe love. The funniest thing I've seen was a woman wearing silver heels and a stylish dark green dress made of clingy material, which made her look like she was wearing a plastic rubbish bag. And those people wearing bright red runners? Fire engine red. Why? Just to stand out? No idea.

There are two main reasons I am writing this. First, there are still about four hours to kill until my train leaves. Because I don't have a phone now, I need a way to fill in time, and do something with my hands. It feels *really* weird not having a phone to look at, it's difficult to just sit here and gaze around. Everyone else sitting in the food hall now, except two elderly ladies chatting, stare at their phones or laptops. Even the teenagers who were being loud are now all looking at their phones. Now and then one of them shows another one something and they laugh out loud, but mostly they are silent, engrossed.

I didn't think I was addicted to my phone, but obviously I was.

It was always with me and was actually a big part of my life when I stop and think about it. The alarm on my phone woke me at 6.00 am every morning, the first thing I would do is read the news. This habit formed during lockdown, when it seemed crucial to know the latest COVID numbers in my city, and how the rest of the world was coping. When I was able to stop doomscrolling, I would play *Pokemon Go*, a fun addiction. After that, I would get up, eat breakfast and do *Wordle* on my phone, because I felt my brain worked better after some solid food.

I didn't do social media, unlike almost everyone I know. *I* didn't want people knowing where I was or what I was doing, and they certainly didn't need to know what I was thinking.

Books would be read on my phone on the tram, during meal breaks when working, when lying in bed at night. Far easier than carting around a solid book, and you can lie down and read comfortably.

Without the phone I feel detached, cut off from the world. In fact though, I am actually much more *in* the world, aware of things around me, which is absolutely the way I need to be right now. Random thoughts and ideas appear from the sky, new ways to improve my plan.

It also feels extremely strange to be writing with a pen on paper after years of just typing on computers. My writing is all spiky, but it *is* slowly improving. This notebook I am writing in is from a nearby newsagent, it's quite thick with a nice purple cover, and I can slide the pen into the wires on the side.

The second, and main reason I am writing this is to keep a record, and write my story down. I got the idea from one of my all-time favourite movies, *The Great Race*, starring Jack Lemon, Tony Curtis and Natalie Wood. In one scene, they are marooned on an iceberg. The hero is writing notes in a diary that he will put into a watertight container to provide valuable information for those who may follow. (The villain's offsider then says to the villain, 'Hey Professor! Why don't you and me get into the watertight container instead?') These words I am writing now, and planning to write, will hopefully provide information for the police about what happened to me, and why, if Z does manage to find me.

It feels fairly safe here for the moment, I'm surrounded by people, but I am mindful of the CCTV high up in the corner. I try not to look at it. Hopefully, my wig makes me look different enough, and my mask shields most of my face. Not many other people sitting here are still wearing masks but a few are, so I don't feel *too* conspicuous. Cleaners and people behind the counters also still have to wear masks in Melbourne at this stage.

So I should probably start with what happened this morning.

It was about 10.00 am and I was slowly walking home from my weekly yoga class, with my friend Melina. The day was sunny but the temperature was only in the mid teens, I shivered a bit in my t-shirt. I'd twisted my ankle, not in the class but walking down the stairs afterwards, so I was limping a little. We had taken a short cut through the park opposite my apartment building, and walked past a man sitting on a bench behind some trees. I recognised Z immediately, a strong looking man in his forties, some grey now in his hair which was cut prison short. His face was leaner and sharper than it used to be. He was extremely alert, leaning forward on the bench, with a large black backpack on. My heart began thumping wildly, but I managed to calmly keep walking.

Z stared closely at us as we walked past, but didn't move. My hair was now platinum, not brown, I was wearing large dark sunglasses, and was a lot slimmer than I had been the last time he saw me. It helped that I was with someone else, and luckily the limp would have changed my walk. Also, I was still wearing my mask from the yoga class. There was enough doubt, he wasn't sure. I was excruciatingly aware of him watching us as we walked past, but he didn't get up and follow.

Once we reached the street I said to Melina, 'Actually, I might go shopping now instead of home.' So we continued on past my apartment building and turned the corner. Melina noticed something was wrong, she asked was I OK? I replied that I was fine, my ankle was just a bit sore, and I would see her next week.

Melina and I parted ways, and I continued on past the shops to the tram stop. I wanted to run, but my ankle was sore, and also I didn't want to attract any attention, so I just walked as quickly as possible. Luckily, a tram was there waiting, climbing on thankfully I sat near a door. The tram didn't leave for what seemed like ages but was actually only five minutes. I kept checking my watch and looking down the road expecting to see Z at any moment, but he didn't show up. Finally, the tram dinged its bell, shut its doors and lurched off. As we picked up speed my heart rate slowed down.

He wasn't supposed to get out for another five years, at least. And I was supposed to be warned. Checking my phone, I was shocked to see that the police hadn't contacted me for about nine months. Up until now, someone had been contacting me every six months or so, just checking in and keeping me updated. Something had gone seriously wrong somewhere in their systems. Was Z responsible for that?

I decided not to call the police, it was too late, what could they really do now? He was out of jail and had already found me once. I *had* thought I still had plenty of time to prepare. Long ago, I had declined the offer of witness protection, not trusting that Z wouldn't be able to find me using his exceptional cyber skills. My plan had been to change my name closer to the time, and then disappear overseas for as long as possible, maybe even forever.

Well, that was impossible now, anyway my passport was back in my apartment. I would just have to do my best by myself, with the current situation. As with most things in life, we really are on our own when it comes down to it, the only person you can truly rely on is yourself. Today is perfect proof of that.

As the tram swayed and clattered towards the city, I rang work and told them I had to fly overseas for a family emergency, didn't know how long I'd be away. They wished me well, approved leave for me, asked me to update them when I knew more. My current job is in admin for a salary packaging company, with an employer that treats me well. I've been working from home since COVID, they *did* want us back in the office now, but left it up to the individual. I chose to stay home. I didn't feel the need to be surrounded by people, pay for lunch, get dressed up, wear makeup every day, commute. I could do my job just as well, if not better, from home. So why wouldn't I want an extra two hours in my day? I chose to work four long days with Mondays off, which was fine with them. I was not that ambitious, I didn't feel the need to network, or drink with managers. I hoped that I would be able to work for them again, one day.

Melina got a similar message via text, I added that I might be uncontactable for a while. She simply sent me her love and wished me luck.

Using my bank app, I paid three month's rent and bills in advance. Why three months? That was the amount of ready money I had in my account, and also I thought it was either long enough for Z to find me, or hopefully, give up looking.

Arriving in the city, my first stop was at the main branch of my bank. I worried that I might not be able to easily access a large amount of cash, which would quickly spell the end of my plan. But it was *my* money after all, I just hoped I had enough ID on me. I'd never been inside this branch before, I just knew it from the outside as a grand, gothic looking pale stone building. Inside was a cavernous space with dark green carpet, an extremely high vaulted and painted ceiling, polished wooden columns, shiny brass fittings. The smell of wax and money.

An elderly man in a dark suit greeted me as I entered, I told him I needed to make a large withdrawal. He smiled, 'Of course!' directing me to wait at a table at the side. Leaning back in an antique chair, I tried not to appear nervous, and gazed up at the mostly golden symbols painting on the ceiling. They appeared to be some sort of crests from the past; sheep, wheat, ships, lions, dragons, unicorns.

Soon, a brisk woman came to attend to me. She didn't seem that impressed by my tracksuit and messy hair. I told her what I wanted to do, she asked for my debit card. When she had checked my high interest second account, her manner subtly improved. I had to fill in and sign a large number of forms, and produce all the ID I had on me; driver's license, Medicare card, debit and credit cards. Luckily that was enough, I was able to draw out my emergency money, $10,000 in cash. I told the woman I was buying a car, she didn't seem that interested. Asking for the money in $50s, it came in two thick envelopes which only just fitted into my shoulder bag.

Leaving the bank, I was again anxious when an insincere beggar approached me. I thought how do you know I've got lots of cash? Then I realised he was approaching everyone who came out of the bank. Shaking my head, I walked around him, trying not to clutch my bag.

Looking back, I was relieved he hadn't followed me, he was now targeting an elderly couple.

Hopping on another tram, I headed towards Queen Victoria Market. Walking up and down the aisles, it took a while before I found the stall I remembered that sold wigs. After trying on a few, I chose a black one with a fringe because it made me look the most different. The stall holder was more than happy to take cash. I also paid cash for a casual jacket with a pattern of black and white palm trees, to go over the plain t-shirt I was wearing.

Using my debit card, I bought a one way ticket on the Skybus to the airport. It was early afternoon by then, the airport crowded and bustling. My card then bought a one way flight to Hobart, the cheapest available ticket to another capital city. I had no intention of flying to Hobart, I just hoped to confuse things a bit, buy some time. That was the last time I used my card, from then on I stayed completely offline.

Walking around the airport, I found the large toilet block that I knew had two entrances. Locking myself in a cubicle, I fitted on the black wig as best I could, and put on the jacket. It was remarkable how different I looked in the mirror, a bit like Cleopatra, or Phryne from *Miss Fisher's Murder Mysteries*. I had the thought, this might actually work. Exiting the toilet block from the other entrance, I hoped anyone looking at CCTV would not think it was the same person that had gone in the other door.

Takeaway from McDonald's was next, I was seriously hungry by now. The chips and burger I ordered were not my usual type of healthy meal at all, but they *were* tasty. I ate too quickly, then discretely placed my phone, which I left on, into the greasy paper bag and scrunched it up. This actually caused me grief, my phone was only a few years old, but it had to be done. The paper bag was then pushed down into a disgusting looking bin.

I paid cash for another Skybus ticket back to Southern Cross Station. Once back there I worked out where to buy a train ticket to Sydney.

My current plan is to hide in plain sight in a giant city, hopefully just blend in and disappear. Which brings me up to date to the present time.

Well, that's killed a few hours, still a couple to go. I might go and buy some clothes in the nearby factory outlet.

I am back. I took my time and bought a whole bunch of things. First I found a silver rolling suitcase, useful to make me look more like a tourist, as well as for carrying my new clothes; underwear, a few cheap t-shirts, a pair of pale blue jeans, and a warm black denim jacket. Trying on jeans filled in quite a bit of time, which was useful. Finally, I found some good black shoes and a reversible dress, because you never know. That should be ample for now, and cover a week in Sydney at least. I've also got the grey tracksuit pants, black t-shirt and black runners that I am currently wearing. My favourite purchase is the reversible dress, it has a completely different colour and pattern on each side, very clever.

Shopping for clothes filled in loads of time, I can go and board the train now.

TO BE CONTINUED

Monday 30 May 2022 9.17 pm

I'm sitting in my compartment on the overnight train to Sydney, the coolly named XPT. There are three seats in the compartment, and I'm sitting next to the window. A detachable little shelf clips handily to the side of the seat, and I am writing on that.

When the gate was opened, the long silver train was waiting, gleaming golden in the sunset. A tall man in a grey conductor's uniform was standing there, importantly holding a clipboard. He smiled professionally, checked my ticket and directed me to the last carriage, which contained the sleeping compartments. Inside this carriage is a long corridor with windows along one side and the compartments along the other. The second compartment is mine, the first contains an Indian family of three; parents and a little girl who smiles at me. Between us is a shared bathroom containing a toilet, basin and shower. The toilet and basin are ingeniously designed to fold into the wall.

On my seat was a towel, as well as a small zippered toiletry bag containing a tiny tube of toothpaste, a folding toothbrush, shampoo/conditioner and body wash. There was also a handy little folding cup for water. Excellent, because I had none of these. A bottle of water and a small pack of soy crisps was also on the seat, which I scoffed down and enjoyed.

A different conductor with a different clipboard knocked and entered my compartment. After crossing me off his list, he confirmed that I had the compartment to myself tonight, I was relieved. Declining to order a hot dinner from him because I wasn't hugely hungry, I did choose coffee rather than tea with my included breakfast. The conductor advised me of the food carriage down the other end of the train, and to call him when I wanted my bed made up. He seemed a bit nervous, I think he was new to the job. I locked the door behind him.

The train departed exactly on time, 7.50 pm, gliding off smoothly. I said a silent goodbye to my brave, cool city full of tough, resilient, multicultural people. My city which has lived through cars mowing people down, random stabbings, one of the world's longest lockdowns. I'll miss the trams, the gothic buildings, my tribe dressed in black. The sirens, the crowds, I love it all! I'll even miss the impossible weather, today was sunny but icy, typical Melbourne. I'm not sure when or even if I'll be back.

Abandoned back in my apartment, food will go off in my fridge, my plants will die. But I feel that I have no choice, I *must* leave right now.

Out of the station, the train picked up speed and zoomed past new apartment blocks that looked like broken teeth, built next to houses old enough to have chimneys. There were a few old grain silos, disappointingly not painted with beautiful murals like you see in country towns. Some abandoned looking, graffitied sheds. Soon we passed through more modern outer suburbia, houses with large driveways and garages built to their boundaries, with little if any lawns.

Not long after that it was too dark to see much, and I was hungry enough to eat something. I carefully made my way along the swaying train, through two carriages of passengers in seats. Some people were already sleeping, most were eating from cardboard boxes of hot food, or watching their devices.

The food carriage didn't have a lot to choose from, but I bought a pack of salad sandwiches and a thick slice of chocolate cake. To drink, I bought three sealed plastic cups of white wine. It was tricky carrying everything back to my compartment, but I managed with a bit of juggling. My meal was tasty enough, and I made the wine last as long as possible.

The ride became rockier. We sped through a few old train stations now and then, lit up a ghostly yellow. But mostly, it was just black outside.

There actually aren't that many people on this train, and only two of the sleeper compartments appear to be in use. The passengers in the seats are spread out, maybe a third of all the seats are occupied. I wonder why people choose to travel overnight sitting up? Mainly to save money I suppose. My sleeper was about the same price as flying, but the seats were actually about half the price. Maybe some people just prefer train travel, or are scared of flying? I chose a sleeper instead of a seat mainly because I wanted more comfort, also because I'd never been in one before and they looked like fun. Another movie I love is *Some Like It Hot*, with Jack Lemon and Tony Curtis again, but this time with Marilyn Monroe. They are all in a girl band, the guys are in disguise. At one stage they travel on a train with sleepers from Chicago to Florida to escape from some gangsters who are trying to kill them. Sort of appropriate really.

I decided not to attempt a shower in the swaying train, I'll have one when I get to Sydney, but I do brush my teeth, which is tricky enough.

I'm feeling OK. A bit drunk, so relaxed, and safe enough because I can lock my compartment door and draw the curtains. Distance is helping too. I'm not really tired, but it's quite late, I should let the conductor make up my bed so that he can finish up for the night.

Tuesday 31 May 2022 2.34am

Trying to sleep on this train is like trying to sleep in a washing machine. I did manage to drop off for a bit, the wine helped, but now its early morning and I'm wide awake. There is a sour taste in my mouth and I can feel a headache coming on. The temperature in the compartment feels too hot now, lights keep flashing by outside.

Getting back to sleep is impossible. I haven't had this sort of sleep problem for years, not since Z was first locked up. In those days I would lie awake most of the night, sleep would completely elude me. It was like my body had forgotten how to do it. The darkest thoughts always appear in the dead of night, by morning, usually it doesn't seem so bad.

I keep seeing Z, sitting there in the park watching my apartment building. I keep thinking that if I'd been walking home along the street, I wouldn't have seen him at all. What had his plan been? Had he already knocked on my door? As I wasn't home, did he then go and wait for me in the park? Would he have followed me and forced his way into my apartment? Maybe he was going to just attack me in the street? Was there a knife in his backpack?

OK, I need to stop thinking like this, so I'll start writing my story.

It's not very comfortable. I don't know how to put the bed back so I'm sitting up in my bunk, my back awkwardly against the wall, the small reading light shining weakly over my shoulder.

This is going to be difficult and painful to write, there are plenty of awful experiences that I don't want to remember, far less put down on paper. But the reason I'm going to do it now is to explain what happened to me in the past that got me to this moment in my life, and why I'm doing what I'm doing now.

Z and I met in a bar when we were in our mid-twenties. I should explain that I'm calling him Z because, like in Harry Potter, I don't want to give him any power by naming him, childish I know. Z for zero, zilch, nothing, because I wish he didn't exist.

We were both single, I was out with my housemates, he was on his own. I'd spilled my drink, he bought me a new one, I was too easily impressed. Z was neat looking without being handsome, had good skin, was not that tall but was taller than me. He seemed somehow completely different to most of the other guys I knew, for one thing, he made me laugh. He took my number and actually *did* call me the next day.

Our first date was in the city on a Saturday night, at a popular, big old-style pub on a corner. The night proceeded extremely well, we laughed, drank, talked a lot as we got to know each other. Z had a dark sense of humour, and seemed unusually intelligent. We discovered that we had an eerie amount in common, and noticed that we even looked a bit similar. We both had lightish brown hair and a similar, long facial structure, but Z had ice blue eyes whereas mine were brown. His skin was pale, mine was olive. Both of us were the only children of migrants, who were now dead; Z's parents had been Scandinavian, one of mine was Mediterranean and the other was Eastern European. We both worked for banks, but different ones, Z was in security and I was in the call centre.

We ended up staying at the pub until closing time, then staggered arm in arm back to my place. The sex was good, he considered my needs as well.

The next morning, Sunday, Z met my housemates. He was polite, but didn't want to spend any time with them. The two of us spent the day exploring the enormous Melbourne General Cemetery, which was a mind-blowing place, I'd never been there before. Z knew it well, showed me the graves of famous people, the grave with a pool table on it, the Elvis Memorial. He showed me graves of Prime Ministers I'd never heard of, statues of Burke and Wills the explorers, the judge Redmund Barry who had sentenced Ned Kelly to hang. For me, the most exciting thing I saw was a fox darting among the graves and disappearing, maybe descending into the underworld.

We had a romantic dinner at a cosy little Italian restaurant in Lygon Street and then parted ways. Z apologised that he had to get up early for work, I was disappointed. When I finally got home my housemates were curious about him and teased me in a friendly way, which made me happy.

Tuesday 31 May 2022 3.05 pm

I wrote on the train until about 4.00 am, I think. By then I was feeling sleepy again and a bit dizzy, so I turned off the light and tried to sleep some more.

There was a polite knock on my compartment door at 6.00 am, I jerked awake feeling awful and very tired. It was a female conductor this time, too cheerful, with the breakfast pack. I found the orange juice refreshing, the cornflakes and milk, not so much. The large coffee was strong, hot and extremely welcome.

Pulling back my curtain, the sky outside was a hazy pink and blue. Our train was zooming past Sydney suburbs with much the same backyards as Melbourne ones; lawns, sheds, seating. A few small above-ground pools. The train didn't stop at any of the nicely kept old-style suburban train stations we were passing through. There seemed to be many more of these than were left in Melbourne, we had "modernised" most of ours. Dozens of city workers were already waiting for their trains at these stations, some sitting on benches, most standing gloomily.

Before too long, our train pulled into Sydney Central Station, and I followed the Indian family down the steps onto the long platform. The little girl was excited, the parents seemed tired like me.

My first impression of the station was of grandeur; an impressive old sandstone building, vintage tiles, high ceilings, archways, a bar with impressive stained glass windows. Strolling around, I got my bearings, read some travel posters. The Information Desk was not open yet but the bar was, so I wheeled my suitcase in there and ordered my second large coffee of the day. I was their only customer.

I chose to sit in a booth under a stained glass window, which was under a tall curved sandstone arch. The top part of the window had NSWGR (New South Wales Government Railways?) written in red glass, underneath were red flowers on curving green stalks, and leaves. Across the bottom was a bright blue hilly line, surely the Blue Mountains. I really like stained glass, and these windows were magnificent. They actually looked brand new, but were probably just extremely well cared for. I was happy gazing at them, not thinking of anything much and letting the time pass. The spell broke when a woman about my age came into the bar and also ordered a coffee, she had bright pink hair and was wheeling a matching bright pink suitcase.

I finished my coffee and approached the Information Desk, a couple of people were now standing behind the counter. They were wearing masks and so was I, but no-one else was. The rather bored looking woman answered my questions about nearby, not too expensive hotels. She directed me to Pitt St, five minutes walk away, showing me on a map.

Leaving the station, I came across a "light rail" stop. Two red carriages, coupled together, were waiting there beneath an awning. I suppose because this is Sydney they couldn't possibly be "trams," because that's what Melbourne calls them?

Wheeling my suitcase down the hill, I was moving against the tide of people streaming up to the station. Compared to Melbourne, these people seem a bit tougher somehow; they don't smile, they walk extremely quickly. If they bump into you they don't say sorry.

I wanted to get off the street as soon as possible, but all the hotels I tried needed proof of ID. One kindly older man, behind the counter at one of the hotels, suggested I try a place around the corner, he thought I might have some luck there. I followed his directions, and sure enough, this hotel I am in now didn't ask for ID, and was happy to take cash. I just needed to fill in a card, which I did with the new name I had thought of for myself on the train, and made up an address, easy as. The reception desk was behind a grim security grill, but the young Asian woman was friendly enough. I booked for a week which should do for now, handed over a lump of cash, no problems. The woman directed me to a tiny, rickety old lift which just had room for me and my suitcase. My room is on the top floor, at the front of the building looking over the street. There is the constant hum of cars and trucks rumbling down below. Sirens now and then. But it feels *so* good to be able lock the door and put up the chain.

First, I had a very welcome and very long hot shower, then caught up on some sleep.

It felt wonderful to put on some clean, brand new clothes. So here I am, sitting on a much more comfortable bed and writing, now and then glancing up at the locked door.

When I met Z, I was living in an old two storey terrace house in Carlton. I shared with two guys and another girl, a good balance. Share houses are great, you get to know your housemates really well, and you get to know all their friends too. There is always someone around to have a drink with. Being an only child, I loved having people my own age around, it was a bit like having brothers and sisters but not quite.

The house was very run down, our landlord was a jerk. He would only fix things if they absolutely needed it, and then do it as cheaply as possible. The fireplaces were crumbling, the showers leaked. This landlord would also drop in unexpectedly, which he was not allowed to do under the law, but he didn't care.

Z didn't spend much time at my place, if we stayed there overnight he always wanted to go out for breakfast. He didn't make much effort to get along with my housemates, avoiding them if he could. Z didn't really understand how share houses worked, he was used to living alone and doing what he wanted, when he wanted. For example, sometimes we would all watch TV together, but decisions as to what to watch were made democratically, and Z didn't always get his way. He would then sulk, or we would leave.

Z lived in Richmond, in a smallish two bedroom older-style flat. He was on the first floor, there was no balcony but it was very close to the city. The flat was kept neat and clean, but there was nothing much in it. No pictures on the walls, no curtains, no books. The main living area had a large TV, and an old orange and brown striped sofa with one matching armchair, with those wooden arms that give you bruises. Z's bedroom just contained his bed, not even bedside tables.

The second bedroom was the computer room. This was a dark, windowless room. I remember the first time I saw it, for some reason I thought of Batman's Batcave. This room contained a large heavy desk, a computer chair and one computer with the biggest screen I'd ever seen, even larger than the TV.

I asked, 'What do you use the computer for?'

'Lots of things, games, chatting to people and also sometimes for work.' He told me his job was cyber security at his bank. That was the first time I'd ever heard that term.

'What's that, what do you actually do?'

He explained, with some pride, that it meant going deep into the bank's online security systems, looking for holes and then plugging them. I must have looked bewildered. He explained that it was specialised work you had to have a talent for, and luckily, he did.

I asked if we could play a computer game. He replied that the games he liked were not really designed for women and anyway, he only had one chair. So I quickly learned that the Batcave was *his* domain.

The furniture in my share house mostly belonged to the other girl, who was a bit older

than the rest of us, I think she was in her thirties.
There was a glass table she owned in the lounge
room that Z would sometimes sit on if we were
alone, mainly because he had been told not to.
One day, as he sat on it, the glass made a loud
cracking noise and broke. He jumped up quickly
and said, 'Let's go.'

Of course, I told everyone what had
happened, assuming Z would pay for it. But he
didn't. He complained, to me, 'It's not *my* table,
why should I pay for it?' I pointed out that he
had broken it. He denied that, said it must have
already been cracked.

Time went by and *I* ended up paying for
the glass, to keep the peace. This annoyed the
others, they thought Z should pay and so did I,
but we were in the honeymoon period of our
relationship where you overlook things.

It became more awkward whenever Z
was at my place. My housemates now actively
disliked him which made it really uncomfortable
for me, in fact for all of us. So we spent most of
our time out, or at his place. When it was just the
two of us, everything was fine, in fact better than
fine. He was funny, romantic, would pay for our
meals which I wasn't used to. But he said he
earned more money, and was happy to spend it
on me. This was all new to me, and I liked it.

After a few months, Z suggested I move
in with him. This was a bit sooner than I was
ready for, but it seemed to make sense, rather
than pay rent for my rarely used room. I thought
it was worth a try. Z was strong and steady, fun
and adventurous to be with. He was also

thoughtful, romantic. He did have his flaws, but I glossed over them, because I wanted to. I'd never lived with anyone before, and I really wanted to experience that.

Z said he wanted to have a child with me one day. The idea of him, me and our child, that perfect triangle, shimmered in the distance.

Friday 3 June 2022 9.10 pm

I bought some supplies on my first day here at this hotel. Donning my wig and mask, I ventured out to a 7-Eleven conveniently situated a few doors down. It had CCTV of course, but I decided I was being too paranoid, how would Z know to look for me right here right now?

There is no fridge in this hotel room, so I wandered the aisles searching for things that would keep, and keep me going for a few days. I ended up buying muesli bars, fresh and dried fruit, nuts, cherry tomatoes, cheese and crackers and two minute noodles. I also bought some red wine and a bottle of scotch, which I drink straight or with water for variety.

I was able to just stay completely in my room for the first few days. I feel a bit like Proust, writing in his bed, hiding from a dangerous world. In his case it was asthma that was the danger, in mine it's Z.

This hotel is small, old and rundown. Probably built for travelling salesmen back in the day. My room is tiny, not designed for long stays at all. There is not even a chair let alone a table or desk. So I sit up on the bed, my back against the wall like on the train, but *much* more comfortable.

A large TV screen is on the wall directly in front of me, a split system high above the windows to my right. One bonus, the shower is larger than usual these days. The bathroom smells mouldy though.

My view is nothing much, just an unexciting grey building opposite with reflective windows, no balconies, I'd say offices. This area has a bit of a dodgy feel to it. There are shifty looking people hanging around, giving you searching looks. The odd syringe lies in the gutter. The area doesn't seem dangerous during the day, however, there are always plenty of normal office people about. I stay in at night.

I suppose I'm feeling safe enough here overall, for now. I need to catch my breath, and plan what to do next. Do I stay here, hiding in all these crowds? I'm not sure yet.

I'm spending most of my time watching *ABC News 24* during the day, which makes the time pass and takes my mind off things. The news itself is depressing, war in Ukraine, interest rates and the cost of living rising. The price of lettuce is ridiculous and is actually a news story. I'm getting to know and like some of the presenters, for example Madeline, she wears unusual clothes and sometimes has an opinion. The weatherman is intelligent and has dimples. During the day I like Joe, who is dapper, and also has an opinion. Another one I like is Greg, always in a grey suit, in the afternoons. Both of these men have faces that look kind. In the mornings, Michael and Lisa are solid and dependable, like parents. I really enjoy listening to Patricia, who pops up to have a friendly chat with Joe mid-morning, even though it's about politics. That's actually the highlight of my day.

The first few days here were a relief, I felt safe and secure and I had time to think. My escape plan seems to have worked, so far, but my whole life is now up in the air, because of Z.

Then I started to feel bored. I put on my disguise and ventured out now and then to stock up on more supplies. But there were too many people swarming everywhere, loud noises, raised voices. I was always looking over my shoulder. There are people here who look like Z. I felt anxious every time I went out, so I mostly stayed in. No-one else seemed to be wearing a mask in Sydney so I felt really conspicuous in mine.

One time I was waiting at some lights, when a young woman started verbally abusing me. She demanded aggressively, 'Where are you from?'

I just said, 'I'm not from around here,' and she spat at me! The woman had long dark hair and a wild look in her eyes. Another time, I almost walked into a youngish man yelling at no one and throwing his phone on the ground so hard that it smashed. I turned around and quickly walked the other way.

So now I need to make a decision about what to do next. I feel stuck, cooped up, scared to go out. I really need to be somewhere else, where I can feel safe. Somewhere less crowded, quieter. Actually, that's given me an idea, I'll go and check.

I was right. Walking back to the train station, I looked around until I found the posters I had seen when I arrived. They are old style, retro or art deco I think? Simple angular drawings in muted colours, the women wear those tight fitting tiny hats and long strings of pearls, the men are in suits and ties. I found the one I thought I remembered, except that the place was actually called Tomakin, not Tomahawk. My memory was close.

The poster asked, "Do you want some peace and quiet away from the crowds? Come and stay at Tomakin Holiday Cabins, right on the beach!" I noted the phone number and luckily there was a free pay phone nearby.

Unfortunately, my initial brilliant idea of getting a "burner phone", or pay as you go mobile hadn't worked out. You needed ID, they were quite strict.

The number rang for a while, then I spoke to a woman. She sounded pleasant enough so I went ahead and booked a cabin for a month, it was *way* cheaper than Sydney. The woman then gave me clear and comprehensive directions to Tomakin. Another good thing about going there is that it will be winter which is their quiet season. So that's where I'm going, no idea what it will be like, but I'm sure it will be better than here.

On Monday I will get the daily 9.00 am bus to Batemans Bay which will take nearly seven hours, and then another bus to Tomakin which takes about 30 minutes. That's OK by me, the trip is mostly along the coast, I don't mind a long, hopefully interesting bus trip. I didn't realise it was so far away, but that's actually good, it should be a safer place to hide for a while. Somewhere I can go and pull up the drawbridge. I'm a bit nervous though, is it a good idea to go somewhere small and be more conspicuous? But I'm also glad to be getting out of here. I've got my ticket, paid for in cash of course, and have packed.

The last few drinks from my bottle of scotch were my celebration, for making a decision, and being on the move again. I feel like I'm back in control of my life.

2003

At first, living with Z was blissful. We were happy in each other's company, we liked to cook for each other. He was actually a talented, innovative cook and enjoyed doing it. I hated cooking but made an effort, and gradually improved. We liked to go out for dinner to small, intimate places in the city or suburbs, and for long interesting walks. We enjoyed day trips into the countryside or down to the Mornington Peninsula in his car. I'd gotten rid of my beaten up Corolla by then, because we didn't really didn't need two cars. It was good to always have someone there to do things with.

Z would mostly decide where we would go and what we would do, I was happy not having to come up with ideas. Now and then I did make suggestions, things that I used to like to do with friends. For example, I suggested we go to the Dan O'Connell, an Irish pub, on St Patrick's Day to drink green beer and play pool. But Z preferred events that just involved the two of us.

He was in love with me, I was absolutely sure of that. He flattered me, said things like I wore colours well, that he was so lucky to have met me. I was a bit more reticent, that's just me, but I did say that he made me feel happy and secure.

Sometimes, when I was having a bath, he would bring me a glass of champagne. He would light a candle for me, then bring in a chair and have a glass with me. I thought that was so romantic.

One weekend, just for fun, we turned off all the electricity and only used candles at night (the stove and hot water were gas so we could still cook and have a hot bath or shower). It was like we were in own little primitive world. We sat on the floor, drank wine and talked about our dreams and hopes for the future. Z saw our future as bright, we would get married, buy a house, have kids, pets, a pool. That *did* sound good to me. He had purpose and goals, whereas I'd just been sort of drifting along. I felt like I had finally found my place in the world, to be with him. We told each other we loved each other, a first for both of us.

You take baggage into any relationship. My handful of previous relationships had all failed, I sort of had that expectation actually. This was Z's first proper relationship, and he was determined it was going to be perfect. I don't know why he chose me, still don't.

We became our own team against the world, our own exclusive club for two. It suited us both, but for different reasons. I liked feeling wanted, safe and secure. He liked having me to himself, always having someone at home, and someone to look after and protect.

Monday 6 June 2022 7.00 pm

I checked out early, it seems like the woman is there 24 hours. I hadn't slept that well, half remembered, confusing dreams waking me. The day was gloomy weatherwise, with a dark threatening sky. I was feeling jumpy, exposed and really keen by now to get out of this big unfriendly city. I'd been to Sydney before as a tourist, but this time I felt more like a fugitive, or a ghost. I'd done my best not to leave any traces, I hoped I'd done enough. Taking off my wig once I'd turned the corner from the hotel, I stuffed it into my bag.

Trudging up the hill with my suitcase, at least I was not fighting the tide this time. After a bit of a search, I found where the bus was leaving from. It was actually *under* the station, an old and hidden away part of the complex.

On the bus, I chose a seat on the left, optimistic for a view of beaches. I was pleased to see that there were TV screens and a toilet on the bus. The TV screens were never turned on at all during the trip, however. The sign on the front of the bus said "Eden," which I took to be a hopeful omen.

The bus was five minutes late setting off, which made me anxious. I was relieved when an older couple appeared and climbed onto the bus, clutching their tickets. They looked lost and confused. I felt for them, I had gotten confused as well.

Sydney traffic was hectic, as always. Our bus drove past intriguing, pale old stone buildings, a castle tower on its own. Buildingwise, Sydney appears to be a sandstone city; grand, light and bright. In contrast, Melbourne is more of a bluestone city; dark, cool and mysterious. We drove through lots of narrow curving streets, containing small old terrace houses with steep overgrown gardens. Then a different style of terrace house with corrugated iron rooves and one cute attic window each, also bungalows with verandas.

I saw many animated signs for VIP Lounges, which I know to be places with poker machines, they seem extremely popular. I actually enjoy reading signs, the weirder the better. I wondered what Glicks could be?

Soon the bus diverted to the airport to pick up one lone passenger. Lots of flying kangaroos on plane tails here. Also lots of construction happening.

Other signs I enjoyed were Benny and the Pets, It's Jerky But Not, and another one to ponder, Thynk.

The bus crossed a large river, I saw a sign to Brighton-Le-Sands, which sounded posh. Grass trees were for sale by the side of the road. Then bushland, a "Low Fire Risk Today" sign, railway lines and very old farmhouses.

I noticed quite a few commuter carparks. I wonder if the road or railway came through first?

More thick bushland, smallish white lilies bowing their heads. Black trunks where trees had been burnt, horses in coats, Sublime Point Lookout which *did* sound nice. Then signs for Shellharbour, Illawarra, I love these evocative names. A Tiny Homes display. A sign for Bombaderry. Soggy looking fields with herds of brown and white cows. A helicopter on a pole.

Early afternoon the bus pulled into Nowra, our lunch stop. There were a few streets of uninspiring shops, I found a café with seats outside undercover. My lunch was a toasted sandwich and coffee, which was strong and woke me up. The rain was constant now and it was quite cool, a good day to be on a bus.

The journey continued, there were Caravans For Sale, more shameful lilies, the cutest little miniature ponies. A small, old forgotten graveyard. Glimpses of the coast.

On the bus, people were starting to play their music; rap at the back from the French backpackers, Fleetwood Mac at the front from the older people.

We drove past logging, Ulladulla, Mollymook. Passengers were now leaving the bus here and there, being picked up or left along with their suitcases. A beautiful malamute and its owner were waiting at one stop, they just picked up a parcel from the bus. We continued on, passing an Ex Servo's Club, yet another Tiny House Showroom, Dolphin Point Tourist Park.

Finally, we pulled into Batemans Bay. I climbed out thankfully, feeling a bit stiff.
It turned out that there was nearly an hour until the next bus to Tomakin, so I explored Batemans Bay which didn't take long. I wondered how big

Tomakin would be, if Batemans Bay was the larger place? There were two main streets, a pub with an upstairs veranda, a couple of young guys leaning on it with their beers, real estate offices, a newsagents. Some clothing/surf type shops, gift shops for tourists, restaurants closed now but open later for dinner. A Club of course at the end of the road, this *is* NSW.

I managed to find a large Coles and stocked up on food for a few days, not knowing what the Tomakin options might be. I got my usual stuff, enough for a week, and another bottle of scotch. There was still time for a gelati from the Ice Creamery, I chose pink grapefruit, and sat outside under an umbrella.

Batemans Bay came across as a nice place. People seemed more friendly than in Sydney, I noticed. They actually smiled at you.

A handful of other people were now waiting for the bus, mostly elderly couples who all seemed to know each other. The driver took cash which suited me and them. I sat in the front so as not to miss my stop.

The much smaller bus rumbled off and drove mostly along the beautiful coastline, it was breathtaking in places. Many small bays with modest houses built to face the views. One bay had a perfect little island at one end. Quite a few of the houses had names on them, like "Sea Breeze." The bus stopped at a few places to let people off, they all seemed to know the driver and gave him a cheery farewell. The road turned inland now and then, I saw one intriguing place hidden away in the bush, with fairy tale towers and turrets.

And then I saw the green sign "Tomakin." The bus turned left off the highway and pulled up at a small roofed bus stop. Thanking the driver, I climbed down with my suitcase.

The driver turned around and called out, 'Nick, it's your stop!'

Nick apologised, 'Sorry, must have dozed off,' and carefully climbed down the steps behind me. Nick was an elderly man, could have been from seventy to ninety years old, with a friendly smile and a fairly strong European accent. He spotted me trying to get my bearings and simply asked, 'Can I help?'

I told him I was going to the cabin park, he gave me clear directions and asked, 'Do you want me to take you?'

'Thank you, I'll be fine.'

He said he hoped I enjoyed my stay. I thought, what a lovely man.

The road I walked along was beside a river, which must go out to sea. A large and busy looking caravan park was there, part of a chain with a resort style pool. It looked great, but there were too many people walking around or sitting around on chairs. I don't think it would have suited me. Next there was a Club, lots of cars parked there, modern and in a great spot on the river. I would have liked to go in and have a drink, but I know you have to show ID. I walked on past a mix of old and new houses, some of the older ones done up a bit, some left alone.

Most houses had verandas on the upper floor. There were no footpaths, everyone must drive. Two pitbulls up on a veranda barked at me in a not too friendly way.

I walked past a closed café with chairs and tables outside under large leafy trees. Then, at the very end of the road, I was relieved to see the faded sign for the cabin park.

Walking through a permanently open and rusty gate, first there was a car park with a couple of cars, a communal area with a barbecue and one old, wooden picnic table, and then a bunch of cabins spread out along a gravel path.

A sign outside the first cabin said Reception. I gratefully climbed up the steps and pushed open the sliding screen door. Inside, a young guy was sitting at the desk, staring at his phone. He was maybe in his twenties, with curly brown hair, a thin moustache and wearing a brown leather wide-brimmed hat. I'm not sure what look he was going for, cowboy porn star? He looked up with a shy smile.

I said, 'I have a booking?' He slid a clipboard across for me to fill in, and asked for my credit card and some ID.

I told him, 'Sorry, my bag's been stolen and I'm waiting for new cards. I've got cash, is that OK?'

He frowned, 'I'll have to check,' and pushed a buzzer on the desk.

After about a minute, the door behind him opened and a woman came in. She was about sixty, short, slight build with curly grey hair and an unsmiling face. Although she was small, she looked quite formidable. The guy told her my story, she gave me a long stare, I must say I quailed a bit. All I could do was hold her gaze and hope for the best.

She said, sternly, and with a slight Kiwi accent, 'You'll have to pay extra cash for the security deposit then.'

I replied, 'That's no problem. I'd like to pay for a month at this stage, if that's OK?' which I think got her over the line.

She sighed, 'Fine. Just show us the ID when you get it.'

I thanked her, I got the feeling we understood each other. This must have been the woman I had spoken to on the phone. I handed over the cash and filled in the form, which got clicked into a folder, no computers here although there was a machine to take card payments.

The young guy grabbed some keys off a hook and led me out along the gravel path. I noticed how quiet it was, apart from the sound of our crunching feet. It was warmer than in Sydney, there was no rain here. A refreshing, slightly salty smell was in the air. Insects were buzzing. Gardens around the cabins were patchy, consisting of straggly native plants and some dusty looking rose bushes. The cabins themselves were sturdy, but tired looking with peeling paint.

The guy said, 'Ooh, you were lucky there, she doesn't usually do that.' I didn't reply.

He continued, 'I'm Jake, by the way. Fran said you wanted somewhere quiet, so you're in the last cabin. Why do you want somewhere quiet, by the way?'

I'd had plenty of time on the bus to think about this, so I was able to tell him that I was a writer and needed somewhere quiet to finish my book.

'Really? What sort of book are you writing?'

'It's a romance novel, you just copy a formula.' I could see I'd lost him.

'Is there any sex in it?' he asked.

'It's implied.' He didn't understand. I clarified, 'Yes, but it's not described.'

'Why not?'

'Because then it would be porn.' He said he didn't read much.

It seemed that only a couple of the cabins were occupied, one had towels hanging on the veranda and I could hear kids inside. An elderly couple were sitting on the veranda of Cabin 5, drinking red wine, they greeted us. We reached the end of the path, and the final cabin which was past a bend and *was* very secluded. I followed Jake up the steps onto the veranda of Cabin 7. Unlocking the door, he gave me the key.

I thanked him, he stood there a bit awkwardly, I think he wanted to keep talking.

I said, 'Great, thanks, see you.' He left at once.

It was a relief to shut and lock the door, and explore my new home. There is one main living/kitchen area with an old grey sofa, a smallish TV on the wall, a kitchen table behind the sofa, and two kitchen chairs. On the table was a clear glass jug containing roses, a nice touch which made me smile. Two internal doors lead to a bedroom at the front and bathroom at the back. The bedroom contains a double bed and an old free standing wardrobe without a door, the bathroom has a basic shower and toilet. The furniture is worn, but looks clean enough, the flooring is vinyl with an old fashioned busy pattern. The only decoration is a painting on the wall between the internal doors, an abstract sailboat.

The kitchen bench has a sink, kettle and microwave but no stove. Fine, two minute noodles again tonight. A tray on the bench contains some packets of instant coffee, tea bags and sugar. A small carton of milk is in the bar fridge under the bench, and in the kitchen cupboards are mismatched dishes, two of everything. One of the kitchen drawers has an ancient Gideon's bible in it.

This cabin has a comfortable, old fashioned vibe. I feel safe, even a bit welcome.

I stored my food away and hung my few clothes in the wardrobe, there were just enough hangers. The kettle was really old, cream ceramic with a black lid. I plugged it in and made myself an instant coffee which I took outside. Each cabin has a plastic table and two chairs on its veranda. Sitting down, I surveyed the scene.

Spectacular views of the beach are visible through the trees, with a small sandy path leading directly to it. If the cabins were not so run down, I could have pretended I was in a plush resort. I decided to pretend that anyway, and that my rather horrible coffee was a single origin cold filtered short black. The chipped "World's Best Dad" mug I was drinking out of didn't really suit that fantasy, though.

Jake was in the distance outside another cabin spreading fresh mulch from a wheelbarrow. He looked up suddenly and waved at me. I waved back. Apart from that, there was no sign of life anywhere, the elderly couple must have gone inside. I sat there, enjoying the warmish evening until the mosquitos got too annoying.

I've been writing this inside at the kitchen table. I'm dead tired actually, it's been a long day of sitting in buses. I'll just have two minute noodles for dinner and an early night.

PART 2

Tuesday 7 June 2022

It was mostly silent here last night, sometimes I could hear faint traffic noise from the highway. Now and then I could hear dogs howling and what sounded like gunshots, but from a long way away. I imagined guys that looked like Jake standing on the back of utes with spotlights, shooting at defenceless creatures.

Finally, I fell into a deep dreamless sleep. Some sort of bird woke me at dawn, but I didn't really mind. I just lay and listened to it for a while, it had a mournful sort of cry.

Water pressure in the shower was low, but at least the water was hot. Breakfast, which I had on the veranda, consisted of a muesli bar and fresh fruit followed by my usual two coffees. The temperature was mild, the sky medium blue and cloudless.

I decided to go exploring. It was a completely different feeling to being in Sydney, where I was scared to leave my room. Here, I am keen to go out.

Following the sandy path through the trees, in a couple of minutes I reached the beach. There was a light breeze, the air was clean and fresh. The waves were stronger than in Melbourne. The bay curved out to the left, and on the right was the river mouth. Directly to my left was a small toilet and shower block with a beautiful, intricate mosaic of a seahorse on the side facing the water. An old pier was a bit to my right.

First, I walked along the pier. The boards were a weathered silvery grey, creaky and broken in places but still safe enough, I hoped. A solitary fisherman was sitting about halfway down the pier, holding a hopeful line into the water. He was on an old canvas chair with an empty bucket by his side, and glanced up at me as I walked past.

'Good morning!' I said cheerily.

He just looked at me, expressionless. His face was deeply weather beaten and tanned under a battered bucket hat. The man was Asian and could have been quite old.

A small white motor boat was tied up near the end of the pier, bobbing gently. It had a tiny cabin and fishing rods sticking up in the back corners. The boat had no name, just a number, and no occupant.

Reaching the end of the pier, I sat on the hard wooden bench that was there, and gazed out to sea. The only noise was the waves slapping against the pier. My mind was empty. But I realised I felt calmer than I had for quite some time. The endless blue-grey ocean was soothing, even healing. I felt like I didn't exist, and that felt good. I just sat there for a while and could have stayed longer, but felt the need to keep exploring.

On my way back past the fisherman, he said, 'Good morning.'

I smiled and nodded and kept walking. I didn't feel like he wanted a conversation, but maybe regretted not saying anything earlier. His greeting lifted my spirits a little more, which had already been lifted by the peaceful emptiness of the ocean.

I kept walking along the bay, on the firm sand down near the water. The bushland here was scrubby and tangled with a few paths going up into it, local shortcuts I supposed. The only other person I encountered was an elderly but fit looking woman in a faded blue tracksuit, walking a blue heeler dog. We smiled at each other as we passed, the dog was jumping at waves and having a great time. I continued on and after about half an hour, reached the end of the bay and turned around. This would be a good daily walk for me I decided; quiet, secluded and unexpectedly beautiful. I had the beach completely to myself on the way back. If the weather was warmer, this would be a great place to swim.

Exploring the rest of Tomakin didn't take long. The café was open now, it sold hot food, cakes, coffee and a handful of souvenirs. I ordered a coffee and macaron from a very young looking girl and sat outside at a table for one under a shady tree. There were actually quite a few customers around me, I think some might have been tourists, but mostly they seemed to be retired locals who knew each other. I got the impression that only some of them lived here permanently, and others were staying at their holiday houses. A red ute pulled up with two friendly black dogs on the back. An older and younger man got out and greeted people sitting near me, and then went in to order. I decided to leave before anyone spoke to me, I don't really want to become known here. On impulse though, I went back in and bought a blue ceramic seahorse on a string, and a lavender candle. No particular reason, except maybe to look more like a tourist.

Arriving back at the cabin park, I walked past Fran on the path. I smiled, she just nodded. It felt good to get back to my cabin. I hung the seahorse on a hook in the bathroom, it gave the room a bit of a lift. Lighting the candle, I decided the smell was a bit too strong, but it did spread a feeling of calm.

I've got enough food for the moment, but soon I'll have to catch the bus back to Batemans Bay for more supplies.

2004

For Christmas, Z bought me my first mobile phone. They were quite a new thing in those days, and still fairly expensive. My phone was red and it folded up. I liked it but didn't really feel I needed it. He'd always had one, Z told me, from the very first big bricks with the pull out antenna. They were the future, according to him and he was so right.

He added, 'Now whenever we're not together, we can always contact each other.'
At the time, it made me feel secure and loved. We called each other every work day on our lunch breaks. After a while, I felt like we ran out of things to say. I suggested we stop but he got offended. So we had to keep doing it. If I was on a late shift, I had to call Z on my way home. He said he worried about me, it was a dangerous world out there at night. I didn't use to think that, but found it *did* make me feel more secure talking to him as I walked home from the tram, in the dark.

Z was mostly in the Batcave on the computer when I got home; he spent a lot of time there doing whatever he did. I was happy enough reading my books. I've always been a library member and usually had a big pile of books to read. Z didn't read books at all. If he wasn't on the computer, he watched TV.

One day, Z summoned me into the Batcave, which was almost unheard of. On the screen was some grainy black and white footage of people lining up at barred windows.

I asked, 'Is this your bank?'

He smiled, 'No, it's *your* bank!' He was waiting for me to catch on.

'How come you have *this* footage?' I asked.

He replied triumphantly, 'I hacked into your bank's CCTV!'

Z explained how lots of businesses have their passwords just as "Password" or "1234," because they are lazy, or so that other members of staff can easily access some of the systems. I did my best to appear impressed, Z was really quite proud of himself.

After that, he would sometimes show me CCTV footage he had accessed of train platforms, or 7-Elevens. One time, he showed me footage of a robbery at a 7-Eleven. It was confronting to watch. The footage showed two young guys, teenagers really, and one of them stabbed the man behind the counter because he was refusing to open the till. I asked Z if he was he going to show it to the police, he told me of course not. He said first of all, they would already have it and anyway, how would he explain to the police about having the footage himself?

I said I hoped the man was OK and the teenagers were caught. Z just shrugged, which shocked me a little.

Wednesday 15 June 2022

This morning, as I set out for my daily walk along the beach, I saw something unusual. Near the pier was a girl, I'd say she was in her twenties, with long brown hair and a slim figure. She was wearing one of those Brazilian bikinis. And there was an older man with a beard, a bit scruffy looking, taking photos of the girl using a fancy camera with a long lens. He was directing her to kneel in the sand, or stand in the water. The girl looked like she was freezing, and apart from that, quite uncomfortable. It could have been because she didn't like passing strangers looking at her, or because of the photographer himself.

I could hear the man chatting to the girl about his wife, who also felt the cold but it didn't bother him, must be something about being female. I wondered if this was some weird kind of flirting technique, where he was trying to reassure the girl by mentioning that he *had* a wife, but was flirting anyway. Of course I could be wrong, but I got the impression that he *was* trying to flirt. And that she didn't like it.

Maybe the girl had paid for, or won a photo shoot? I don't think they knew each other, and she was much too shy to be a professional model. The chemistry between them was really bad, I felt sorry for her.

The photos would have been stunning, though. Being early in the day, the sun was low and sparkling on the water. The girl had a perfect figure for the bikini, which is rare. Most girls wearing them usually had at least some flab, but she had none at all. The bikini was orange and she had a golden, even tan.

The two didn't look like locals, most likely Canberrans, or maybe even from Sydney. I'd never seen that sort of bikini, or in fact *any* bikini on Tomakin beach before. People did go swimming now and then, but they had grey hair and wore wetsuits.

When I got back from my walk, they were just finishing up. He was packing his camera and she was shivering in a robe. A crowd had gathered by now. I spotted Jake, who should have been at work. He saw me and came over.

'Would you wear something like that?' he asked.

'No, would you?'

He didn't know how to take that, but decided to laugh.

2004

I enjoyed my job in the bank's call centre, I liked talking to people, you never knew what they were going to say. There was always something new to learn, the job had enough variety to stay interesting, at least to me. Most of us working there were in our twenties, a few were a bit older. Some were gay, some were from overseas, most people were outgoing and fun. Sort of goes with the job.

It was a tradition to go to the pub every Friday night after work, and we had a regular table in the basement bar next door. When I first moved in with Z, I invited him along to these nights. Lots of other people brought their partners or friends, and I was pleased that I now had someone to bring. But it turned out that Z didn't behave well in a crowd. He would flirt with the women and disagree with the men. He had some sort of need to dominate which rubbed people the wrong way.

So I tried going without him, but that didn't work. Z would call me, ask me when I thought I would be getting home, always wait up for me. Then he would interrogate me about my night, did I talk about him? I said of course not, although sometimes I did. He would ask me what we talked about, and would criticise people he didn't know, saying things like, 'He really said that? How ignorant!'

I would try and defend people, but that was a waste of energy and would lead to arguments. I could never change Z's mind, and he didn't like me disagreeing with him. I wanted to keep going out with my co-workers, but it became too much of an issue. Z even accused me of preferring my co-workers over him. I could not convince him that he was wrong, so in the end, I just stopped going.

Z never went anywhere himself socially without me, and had no friends of his own. At all.

Apart from my workmates, I did also have other friends in those days. Not many, but a few. Z didn't like me going out without him, so if I planned to catch up with friends, I felt like I would have to invite him along as well. Z saw these nights differently. He thought their sole purpose was so that he could meet (and give his approval of) my friends. More often than not, these nights would not go well either.

Z liked to get into arguments and create scenes. One time he told my friend Cherie that he thought the Dalai Lama was a conman. She got really upset. Cherie was a big fan of the Dalai Lama and I actually was too. Both of us had both gone to see him once when he gave a free talk at the Tennis Centre in Melbourne. Thousands of people were there and it was an inspiring event to attend, we had both been tremendously impressed by the Dalai Lama. I thought he was funny, kind, insightful, strong. He talked for a while and then answered questions from the audience. He always had an answer, no matter how difficult the question. Often it was just a very simple, logical answer. For example when asked by an elder indigenous person how to keep their young people positive about the future, the Dalai Lama said something like, 'Just stay positive yourself.'

Cherie and Z had a loud, heated argument, I didn't feel like I could say anything. Later, when Z went to the toilet, she had asked how I could be with someone who thought like that? I really had no answer for her. I didn't even know if Z *did* really think like that about the Dalai Lama, or just wanted an argument.

Unsurprisingly, my friendship with Cherie lapsed. Gradually, other friends faded away after similar incidents. As time went by it seemed to me that my friends belonged to my past, and Z was my future. He kept reinforcing how much better my life was now, I was secure with him. *He* would always be there for me unlike friends who were fickle, *he* wasn't going anywhere. One person did say I needed other people in my life, not just Z. I agreed in principal, but didn't actually do anything about it.

Sunday 19 June 2022

It's definitely winter now, the temperature gets quite cold at night. The only heating in my cabin is one of those old radiator bar heaters you turn on by pulling a string. It's on the wall in the living area, but there isn't one in the bedroom, which consequently feels like a fridge. So now I'm wearing my tracksuit to bed. The days are generally cool or cold, with the odd mild one thrown in.

Markedly less people are about now in Tomakin, barely any tourists at all. The cabin park rarely has another guest. The caravan park is less than a quarter full and is all grey nomads, sitting on their deck chairs in warm clothes. The café doesn't have many customers either these days, sometimes it's only me.

I've done some touristy things in the area. An interesting boat cruise goes up river, under the Batemans Bay bridge, which actually lifts up. Local craft markets happen at Batemans Bay and Moruya. The Batemans Bay one is smaller, and is only on the first and third Sunday of each month. Moruya's market is larger, and is on every Saturday. I try not to buy stuff, but have bought some jewellery and clothes. Also local gin and honey, both extremely tasty.

But by far the most amazing thing I've done was to hand feed a tiger today.

I knew there was a private zoo not that far away, I'd picked up a brochure about it from a tourist shop in Batemans Bay. The brochure had a map, and the zoo appeared to be relatively near Tomakin, although the map was not to scale.

This morning started out warmer than usual, so on impulse, I decided to try walking to the zoo. I thought if it turned out to be too far away, I'd just turn around and come back. It'd still be a walk, just somewhere different to the beach.

So off I set armed with my water bottle along the bush-lined inland road. No footpath existed but it felt safe enough to walk on the side of the road. Very few cars went by. It took me about an hour but I reached the zoo, I was hot and sweaty by then.

A surprisingly large number of animals lived in this zoo; different types of monkeys, red pandas, otters, giraffes and zebras. Also white lions, tigers and cheetahs. The only other human visitors were an excited young couple, I think they were Chinese, taking loads of photos and smiling selfies. I was happy enough to take some photos for them, but then they wanted a photo with me which I politely declined. After seeing every animal on display, my mood was upbeat. The animals all seemed healthy and well cared for.

In the gift shop, while buying an ice cream, I spotted a sign advertising "Hand feed a tiger here TODAY!" It was not at all cheap, but I thought about it while I was enjoying my rainbow Paddle Pop. When would I get another chance for an experience like this? I decided yes, I really want to do this. So I enquired, they were quite pleased, said not many people did it.

The tiger keeper came out and greeted me, she was a woman about my age wearing a green uniform and had a South African accent. She led me through a locked door, down a tunnel and into the outdoor back area. Between us and the tiger were strong iron bars and wire mesh. I could see him reclining grandly in the shade, but he got up and walked towards us as soon as he saw us. The keeper explained that this tiger wasn't on display because he had a withered leg due to a disease. Buy apart from that, he was in good health and could still earn some money for the zoo like this. His name was something like "Quinoa."

Up close, the tiger was enormous, beautiful, powerful with big white paws and golden eyes. I didn't really notice his damaged leg at all. The keeper brought out a metal plate with a few lumps of raw meat on it, and showed me how to hold them up to the wire so that he could grab them with his teeth.

It was scary the first time Quinoa actually took some meat from my fingers, but I quickly got used to it. His face was really close to me, his fangs were almost as long as my hand, it was an incredible experience. I fed him all the meat on the plate, when he saw there was none left, he just turned and strode majestically back to his shady spot, and plonked himself down.

I was on such a high as I walked back to Tomakin, I felt like I'd conquered Everest or something. I was also happy that Quinoa, "damaged" as he was through no fault of his

own, could still enjoy the rest of his natural life
span.

2004

The second year or so of my relationship with Z, things were still going fairly well for us, we seemed to have settled into being a couple, something I'd always wanted. Our lives were just drifting along, but not really moving forward. So I asked him about getting married, having a baby. He said all in good time, there was no rush to have a baby, he wanted me to himself for a bit longer. Regarding marriage, he said he had no one to ask to be his best man.

We opened a joint bank account because it made things easier, and also because Z was better at managing money. Both our salaries went in, and he paid the bills. A percentage went into a high interest savings account and, in theory, the rest was for us to spend. But if I wanted to buy anything for myself, like shoes for example, I had to explain why.

Z would exclaim, 'You've already got shoes!'

He had a temper, which was like a slow burn that would suddenly erupt in flames. One day we were in a busy pizza restaurant in Carlton, and were waiting longer than usual to get served. I could feel Z getting more and more annoyed, then he stormed out leaving me sitting there. I could feel all the eyes on me. Z didn't come back so I felt like I had to apologise to them, creep out, find Z and calm him down.

Also, while we were driving, he would yell suddenly and scarily at other drivers doing the "wrong thing." Most times they couldn't hear him of course, but it made *me* jump. I said he scared me when he yelled, he explained he was only letting off steam. I got used to it in time, not that I thought it was right.

Something else I recognised early on was that Z was sometimes completely wrong about people, or would take them the wrong way, or see things that were just not there. Z could never admit or even contemplate that he could possibly be wrong, even if there was evidence to the contrary. Once he had made up his mind, it was set in stone. For example, he had been convinced that one of my male ex-housemates was gay. Z said it was obvious from the way the guy talked, his mannerisms.

I disagreed, 'He's not gay, I've met his girlfriend.'

'Just because he's got a girlfriend doesn't mean he's not gay.'

I said that didn't even make sense, Z said I was so naïve.

Here's another example. The apartment building we lived in consisted of eight apartments in total, four on the ground floor and four above, where we were. Tenants were mostly young couples or singles, but then an elderly man, a retired widower named Don, moved in. He was on our floor but not quite next to us. Don was friendly, kind, would do things like take our bin in for us. One day I was chatting to Don on the stairs, when Z appeared.

Don greeted him and then said, 'Well I'd better get going,' and left.

To me, that was Don being considerate because, now that my boyfriend was here, I would want to concentrate on him. Old fashioned, in fact. However, Z saw that as Don not wanting to talk to him because Don didn't like him.

When Don invited us over for dinner soon after that I said, 'See, he does like you.'

'He's just pretending to like me so that he can spend more time with you.'

Mind you, Don was in his late seventies, I think. We didn't end up going over for dinner, and lost that potential friendship, like many others.

Thursday June 2022

The garden upgrade here at the cabin park is more or less finished now. Jake has done an excellent job, I'll give him that.

First, he removed all the existing scruffy plants and weeds and then spread lots and lots of mulch into the garden beds around the cabins. That took him weeks. There are two colours of mulch; a natural sort of rusty red, and also black which adds contrast. Jake spread the mulch out in alternate curving shapes. Concrete statues were added here and there, not *too* many, and a few bird baths. Some of the statues are the thin Buddhas, not the fat ones. Other statues are girls carrying water jugs on one shoulder. New solar lanterns and path lights are now dotted about.

Finally, the plants went in. First were young feathery palm trees which will grow very tall I'm sure. Then other smallish trees which I actually know the name of, Magnolia Little Gems. I love those trees, they have a pleasing round shape with dark green glossy leaves which are brown underneath. In spring and summer they have creamy, vanilla scented flowers.

Filling the gaps are smaller, tropical looking plants. I really like the bright crimson ones, their label says Bloodleaf Plant. Another one I like is called Tricolour Stromanthe, which has unusual leaves that are cream and green on top and bright pink underneath. Finally, planted along the fence line is star jasmine, just dark green now but I know it will have fragrant white flowers in spring. Eventually, when the jasmine covers the fence it will look spectacular, but that will take a few years.

Overall, the garden has a lush, tropical feel. It looks Balinese to me.

I went to Bali once, with Z. He was not the sort of person who wanted to travel overseas, he preferred staying in his home country and mostly staying inside in his own home. Z didn't see the point of travel and thought the cost of overseas flights was ridiculous. But there was also another reason he didn't want to fly.

I *loved* to travel, I'd been backpacking in Europe in my early twenties which was life changing. Marvelling at an ancient castle on an island, in the middle of a lake with white swans, was truly like being in a fairy tale. A month in Thailand and a Pacific cruise were other things I'd done. My favourite place of all was Thailand, the "Land of Smiles." I loved the calm, peaceful nature of the people who never seemed to get angry, as well as the stunning beaches of warm, aqua water and white, powder-like sand.

Z won a raffle at work; a Qantas prize of flights and accommodation for two at a resort in Bali. I was super excited, I'd never stayed in a resort before, it all sounded very swank. But Z put off using the prize until his work told him he had to use it or it would expire. So he reluctantly made the booking. On the day of the flight, he drank more than usual at the airport and swallowed some sleeping tablets, even though it was a daytime flight. At take off, he clutched the arms of the seat so tightly that his hands went white. I was surprised and asked was he scared?

Through gritted teeth, he growled, 'Yes!' I wondered why he hadn't told me, but knew he didn't like showing or admitting to any weakness. He did go to sleep for most of the seven hour flight which was probably the best thing for him.

Once we landed Z felt better, although groggy from the tablets. Immediately he complained about the humidity and grumbled about having to wait in a long disorganised line at the airport.

Luckily we had a transfer to the resort arranged, but as we were driving through the streets lined with shops and stalls Z exclaimed, 'Look at all this cheap junk everywhere, who would buy this stuff?'

I was embarrassed because our driver was a friendly local, Z was oblivious.

Z *was* impressed when we reached the resort however, we were welcomed and treated almost like royalty. Z liked that. After we had checked in, a softly spoken young woman in a beautiful emerald-green silk dress led us to our suite, which was actually a beautiful little "hut" set in a lush garden. A number of similar huts were spread out around the resort, on grassy slopes, a discrete distance from each other. Tall palm trees provided swaying shade, the air had a faint, sweet floral scent.

To get to our hut, we had to cross a couple of little wooden bridges over softly flowing streams. These streams fed into an extensive pool with a bar in the middle of it that you swam up to. The sound of gently running water was everywhere, creating a tranquil atmosphere.

Our hut had an enormous bed with a hamper on it containing a bottle of expensive champagne, chocolates, nibbles and a hand written card saying "Welcome to your new home!" A large TV screen, which provided movies and cable programs, hung on the wall above the bed. There was 24 hour room service.

The first few days we just stayed in the resort. Apart from the pool bar, there was another bar and restaurant with delicious food, both western and local. Z was more relaxed than usual, it was great.

I liked the resort too, loved it in fact but I wanted to explore. To me the whole point of going overseas is to experience other cultures. Z finally reluctantly agreed, so we ventured out of the resort gates the next day. Straight away we were bombarded by a swarm of people waiting there to sell us stuff; tours, t-shirts, jewellery etc.

I was used to this from my other travels and just said a polite, 'No, thank you,' to the would-be sellers. I could tell Z was taken aback and actively disliked the hard sell. He just looked through the people and brushed past them rudely.

He complained, 'They should be banned!'

'They're just trying to make a living,' I tried to explain.

There was no shade on the road to town, the bright sun beat down heavily on us. Z said he felt like he was getting heatstroke after only a few minutes.

I offered him my hat, he said, 'It's purple!'

'So what?'

'People will think I'm gay!'

'So what?'

He didn't answer. A mangy stray dog followed us for a while, then another dog came and the two of them fought quite viciously.

I exclaimed, 'The poor things!'

'They should be put down.'

After about 20 minutes we reached the village, once again there were lots of street sellers and spruikers saying come into my shop or restaurant. Z wanted to buy a hat but found it hard to decide, and hated having to bargain. In the end he just paid the asking price for a plain straw hat one but then of course was really annoyed to see exactly the same hat cheaper, further on.

Our plan was to have lunch in the village, but Z thought the open air bars and restaurants should have air conditioning, and he said they all looked dirty. Finally we found one he approved of, it was more upmarket than the rest with glass doors and did have air conditioning. We had our lunch there, the food was excellent but the bill was horrendous, double what it was at the resort.

Z was in a very bad mood when we left the restaurant, and of course we were surrounded by street sellers again. I knew the anger had been building up all day, but the explosion, when it came, was right off the charts.

He yelled, in a truly fearsome voice, 'NO! A thousand times NO, go away and leave me ALONE!' right into the face of some poor young girl. She started to cry. I was shocked, I don't think I'd ever seen Z that visibly angry before, it was like he wanted to murder someone.

People stared, I felt terrible and a nearby tourist said, 'Hey man, take it easy!' Z told him to mind his own business, but the other guy was much bigger than Z so Z backed down pretty quickly. Our day was ruined, however.

Z stormed his way back to the resort, I practically had to run after him, and he actually didn't leave the resort again until we went home.

Z tried to change our flights and go home earlier, but there were no seats on flights with Qantas available, and he flatly refused to fly with anyone else. He spent the rest of the holiday watching movies on our large TV, or drinking moodily by himself by the pool. If I went and sat next to him and ordered a drink for myself, he would just finish his own drink and go back to our hut without a word. Mostly we ordered room service for dinner, Z didn't even want to go to the restaurant anymore and deal with other people.

He was just enduring the hardship of this holiday like a martyr, that was his attitude.

I did my best not to let Z ruin *my* holiday. Going out by myself, I looked through the shops, bargained, bought stuff. I went on a couple of day tours, to the Monkey Forest and to Ubud. Because Z wasn't with me, I didn't feel stressed at all while I was out. Z of course didn't speak to me when I got back to the resort.

On the last day of our holiday, I got my hair braided. I really liked it, the young girl took a long time and did a fantastic job, I thought. Z just asked why on earth would I want to look like a native? I ignored him.

There was a whole lot of ignoring going on during that holiday.

Monday June 2022

I find I've settled into a routine, more or less. A walk along the beach occurs most days; sometimes early in the morning, sometimes in the late afternoon, but usually at the warmest time of the day, around 2.00 pm. Walking is no fun if there are storms or heavy rain however, so I skip it on those days. Mostly the weather is fine, although the temperature is low. My walks are consistently enjoyable, there is nothing quite like having a stunning beach completely to yourself. In the early morning, sometimes the sand is pristine except for some perfect paw prints, in cute little groups of four. I picture some dog on its own, running as fast as it can.

My notebook is with me wherever I go, and I've hidden my cards. Probably I should have got rid of them completely, but they are extremely difficult to replace and I might need them suddenly. My remaining cash is hidden offsite.

Twice a week or thereabouts, I catch the bus into Batemans Bay for supplies. Sometimes I allow myself a treat and enjoy a meal at a café or one of the restaurants on the river there.

My writing is done at my kitchen table in the cabin. Sometimes the words just flow smoothly, sometimes they don't flow at all. It *does* seem to be getting easier the more I write. Does this mean I have actually become a writer? Without really meaning for it to happen? Originally I was writing to keep a record and to fill in time, but now it's become addictive.

Writing also keeps me sane. If I wasn't writing, I think I might be bored out of my skull. Plus, writing is good for loneliness, takes you mind off it.

When I first came to the cabin park, I used to write outside on the veranda. That was partly to show people that I actually was a writer, but there were too many distractions. Mainly Jake, who would do unnecessary gardening nearby, and chat, he was like an annoying mosquito. I also wanted to avoid Fran, being worried she would ask if I'd got the ID yet. But as time went on, that didn't happen and I ceased to think about it.

When I've finished writing for the day I sometimes watch the news channel, but not as much as I used to. At night I am happy enough staying in and watching Nordic Noir on SBS, or some British crime show on the ABC. After a while, these programs all sort of blur into the same thing; a pair of mismatched detectives, one of each sex, who don't like each other to begin with. Maybe one of them has an addiction, or a child, or some sort of secret. Their boss is usually grumpy. However, by the end of the series they always seem to bond and manage to catch the baddie. Unless there is a Season Two. I enjoy the sound of different languages or accents, and watching stunning, often snowy scenery. It's a useful escape into another world for a while.

Reading books is another enjoyable pastime. A modest "free library" box, shaped like a little house, is perched on a pole near the

Tomakin café. You never know what sort of books will be in that, I've found all sorts; children's books, travel books, cookbooks. Usually I just try the novels, and I always return them. Sometimes there are free lemons as well.

My current non-plan is to remain at the cabin park for three months, under the radar, and finish my story. I'm not thinking any further ahead than that, though of course I should. If I just stay here indefinitely I'll run out of money, but I'll worry about all that later.

Living here is a bit like being in lockdown again; staying inside most of the time and not talking or interacting with many people. The only ones I regularly speak to are Fran, Jake and the café owner, whose name I don't even know.

I didn't really mind Melbourne's long lockdowns too much, although of course they were terrible for many people, I know that. Hundreds died or got very sick and those times were especially hard on teenagers.

It was fortunate that I was one of those people with a job that could be done from home. For years, people at my company had been asking if they could possibly work from home, if they had young kids, for example. They were always being told, no, sorry, it's too difficult, not secure enough, the systems would have to be modified which is too expensive, etc. Well, guess what? When we *had* to work from home because of COVID, or close the business, they worked out how it could be done in less than a week. Packing up all our stuff on our final day in the office felt to me like the end of the world was coming, and we were preparing to descend into some underground bunker, maybe to never re-emerge.

Life became simple. You didn't have to think about should I do this, should I go there, should I catch up with so and so, should I go into that shop and try that on? Those just weren't options. What you wore didn't matter at all, because no one saw you. There was no need to wear makeup, shoes or even pants. You worked, you walked, you went shopping for essentials, you watched TV, you drank. Online shopping became a fun obsession for many of us. If I wanted a purple t-shirt for example, I would spend a long, enjoyable time online, searching for exactly the right one. It would take maybe a month for the t-shirt to arrive from China, and it would cost only $3.00. Going to the mailroom to get your parcel, you might actually encounter a neighbour, and have a chat with a real person. When you *did* come across other people out and about wearing their masks, there was this unspoken, fellow feeling that we were all in this together. Of course, there were some idiots around who didn't wear masks, or wore them on their chins. I didn't waste my energy getting annoyed at those people, I just hoped natural selection would take care of them.

Shortages occurred in those early days which were caused by people stocking up and then stockpiling items. Two people were filmed in a shop having a physical fight over the last pack of toilet paper. Supermarket shelves became bare, which *was* scary. Masks were difficult to get, therefore lots of people bought or made cloth ones you could wash and reuse. Like many people, I set up an emergency shelf consisting of items like pasta, sauces, noodles, cans of vegetables as well as precious toilet paper.

Most shops just closed down. A bar near me had a sign in the window, "NO MONEY, ALCOHOL OR TOILET PAPER KEPT HERE!" No point in breaking in, then.

Restaurants, cafes and bars that *did* remain open were required to offer takeaway, so I would sometimes buy a takeaway cocktail and sip it during my walk. I was by no means the only person doing that.

Early on, there were dark days when the COVID numbers just kept getting worse and there was no vaccine yet. It was like we were fighting an invisible enemy, and that enemy was winning. Once or twice I lost hope, a truly terrible feeling. It became vital, for some reason, to watch Premier Dan's daily press conference around 11.00 am every morning. The urban myth was that the daily COVID numbers could be predicted based on which jacket he was wearing. If he was in his black North Face one, it might be good news. If he was in a suit, it was likely to be bad.

The CBD of Melbourne became deserted, which had never happened before in my lifetime. Venturing there was a surreal experience, like being in one of those movies about the end of the world where only one person was left alive, and that person was you. It felt like tumbleweeds should be blowing through the streets.

I did make that journey now and then to donate blood, which was allowed, and a valid excuse to get out of the house. It was also a chance to talk to real people, even feel the touch of another person. Giving blood was more important than ever during COVID, and it makes *you* feel good as well. Mostly, I would be the only person on my previously standing room only tram. Trams did continue to run, but the drivers were fenced off with tape for their own safety.

Most people *did* find sneaky ways to catch up with friends. Melburnians were only allowed to leave home for four reasons; to go for a walk, shopping for food and essentials, for work or for medical reasons. Going out to socialise was strictly forbidden. I live near the beach and would meet my friend Melina there, on the old pier. Melina is a nurse, and she told me horrific stories about COVID, about intubation. She found it ironic that people complained about having to wear masks for an hour or so, she had to wear one all day, it would get wet and she was mostly too busy to change it.

Melina and I would pretend we were going for our individual walks, had just run into each other by accident, and decided to sit down for a moment on a bench to rest. Little did anyone know that our drink bottles contained wine, sometimes cocktails. Watching a spectacular sunset over the old wooden pillars of the pier was rare magic we craved.

Now that vaccines are freely available, and we have more or less learned to live with COVID, those times seems like a foggy distant memory. I still remember Melbourne's first double donut day of no deaths and no new cases, I actually went out and bought donuts to eat, and I don't even *like* donuts. It's always amusing talking to people from other states or even country Victoria who only had brief lockdowns lasting a few days at the most. They think *they* had it tough, they have NO IDEA.

It's ironic that I have more or less voluntarily put myself back into lockdown again. Fortunately, I already know how to cope with staying inside and not talking to real people. There are other options available to me now of course, I can actually go anywhere and do anything I want. But, I feel better being hidden away here, no one bothers me and I feel safe. Lots of retirees live in Tomakin and Batemans Bay, who prefer to use cash, so I fit right in. I think by accident, I've stumbled upon the perfect place to disappear to. Tomakin is just the sort of quiet backwater I've been looking for. I don't mean backwater in a bad way at all, I just mean that it's peaceful, tranquil. Places like Lightning Ridge or Broome are known places where people go to hide. I don't think most people have even *heard* of Tomakin.

June 2022

My cabin is cleaned when I go out for my walk, and there are always fresh towels when I get back, sometimes fresh flowers. I've tried to tell Fran I don't really need fresh towels every day, but she said she "has her standards." Now and then she is still there vacuuming when I get back, and I wait outside. It's a bit tricky for her because unlike her other guests, I am in the cabin most of the time, writing. But nothing is said. She doesn't say much to me at all in fact, which is fine.

One day, I noticed that the towels had not been changed when I got back from my walk. I wondered if Fran had decided to not change them every day after all, but thought I should just check. Taking a deep breath, I made my way to the office. Fran was sitting at her desk, a cup of tea in hand as usual. I enquired about the towels, she just sighed and told me Jake is doing the cleaning now and must have forgotten them. Standing up, she disappeared into the back room and fetched some clean towels for me. She promised to speak to Jake.

As a result of that, he is not doing the cleaning any more. Now he has started painting the cabins, which will be an extensive, time consuming job. First, all the old paint has to scraped and sanded off. The colour being removed was white, now the cabins are going to be pale lemon, with shiny black trim, which *does* look brighter and fresher. Empty cabins are being done first, I hope it will be a long time until it's my cabin's turn. Only Cabin 4 has been completed so far, and I think that took about a week.

Jake is mostly up a ladder these days, and not doing a very good job, at least in Fran's judgement. He gets told off quite a bit. One day I was at my table writing, when I heard some loud yelling outside. Curious, I went outside and saw that Jake had spilled a tin of yellow paint on the path, and Fran was shouting angrily at him. His face was crimson. I felt a bit sorry for him then, Fran can be fearsome.

2005

Unlike the photographer on the beach at Tomakin, Z excelled at flirting. When I first met him he would flirt with any female, any time and was clever about it. He would say things like, 'That's a very perceptive comment,' rather than 'You look good in that tight dress,' for example.

First of all, I think that flirting has its place, when it's welcome and mutual and between equals who are free. But I think it's genuinely cruel if it's done in front of your partner.

There is no right thing to do if your partner flirts with someone else while you are there. If you just ignore it, people think you are weak or too stupid to notice, or even that you accept it and don't mind. On the other hand if you say something, *you* are the one making a scene. You could leave the venue, but that only works if the other person runs after you, they also might just stay there and keep flirting. I suppose you could try and flirt too, but that's just silly.

It shows a total lack of respect for the other person's feelings, and often also embarrasses the person being flirted with. I explained this to Z, how it made me feel when he did it with my work colleagues or friends. At first he insisted he wasn't aware of doing it, and anyway I had nothing to worry about, *I* was the one he loved, it was just a bit of harmless fun. I said it upset me, and often embarrassed the other person as well. He seemed startled, like the thought had never occurred to him, and possibly it hadn't.

I told him about one time I had seen it happen in Thailand. I was at an outdoor restaurant at night, on one of the islands. Long tables had been set up, a western guy was sitting with a beautiful Thai girl, and there was a bottle of champagne in an ice bucket in front of them. This guy spent the whole night flirting with a drunk redheaded girl sitting next to him on the other side. The poor Thai girl was just left sitting there, ignored and upset. She didn't leave, maybe she couldn't. I don't know if she was a paid escort, or the guy's girlfriend but that was not the point. The point was the public humiliation of her.

Z understood what I was saying, and his behaviour *did* change when I was with him, which proved to me that he *was* aware of it. But, I often wondered, what about when I wasn't with him?

One night we were home, both of us relaxed and extremely drunk, and were talking about the deep-seated nature of human beings. Z actually revealed to me how he liked to play mind games with people sometimes, to find and exploit their weaknesses. He said it was like flirting, sometimes he liked to get the attention and interest from a woman, and then if she said or did anything back, he would appear shocked, like nothing was further from his mind. Of course, this would confuse and embarrass the woman, she would then think she had got it totally wrong. And Z would just sit back and enjoy her embarrassment. I was really surprised he admitted that to me, normally he kept his cards much closer to his chest.

The next morning, when I asked him if it was true, he said he couldn't remember saying anything like that. And if he did he was just making it up, he would never actually do anything like that, come on.

It's ironic that Z would often accuse *me* of flirting, when I never did any such thing. This happened right from the beginning of our relationship, but I just took it as a joke in those early days. For example, if I smiled at someone making me a coffee, Z would say something like, 'He's a bit young for you, isn't he?' and I would just laugh.

When I first met Z, I was having private weekly swimming lessons. My swimming ability was basic in that I could stay afloat, but I had never learned how to do the breathing properly, so that's what I was learning. Z agreed that the lessons were an excellent idea, he was a skilled swimmer himself, but when I mentioned in passing that the teacher was male, Z quickly changed his opinion. He said *he* could teach me, and I should stop paying for lessons. So I did. Z turned out to be a hopeless teacher, he had no patience and would get fed up that I couldn't understand what he wanted me to do. Not that he explained clearly. Anyway, we both knew the lessons with Z weren't working out so I suggested I go back to my former lessons. Z then said something really strange. He said that he thought a female teacher would be a better fit for me, it made much more sense. It actually made no sense at all and my male teacher had been fine, so I went back to him.

Well. Z came to watch the lessons, made sure to be standing there to hand me my towel when I got out of the pool. He said he was just making sure my teacher didn't "try anything."

In the early days of our relationship, we would often go out to pubs and talk to other people, usually it was fine but I was aware that Z did keep a close eye on me and who I talked to. Sometimes that was a good thing. One time a drunken guy put an unwelcome arm around me and Z was there, quick as a flash, and strong-armed the guy right out of the pub. When Z came back in people praised him, but he was asked to leave by the publican because he had been physical with someone.

As we were walking home, in an accusing tone, Z asked what I had been saying to the guy. I replied that I had just been being polite, as women are taught to do, but Z was adamant, I must have encouraged the guy in some way.

End of June 2022

I wouldn't say I'm an alcoholic, but it does take the edge off. After a long day at work, it's always been my reward. Having a drink by yourself can be genuinely enjoyable, and is the next best thing to having a drink with someone else. Sometimes it's better. In my twenties I used to drink a lot, I was a binge drinker. Now I'm just a regular drinker, having one or two drinks per day, I've been doing that for decades. Five o'clock is always wine o'clock for me. Then I have a drink with dinner. Sometimes, I might have a nightcap as well.

I don't see the amount of alcohol I consume as being a problem, smoking is surely much worse for your health. But I do need my daily alcohol. If I'm away on holidays somewhere, I have to make sure I have at least *some* alcohol in the fridge, panic if I don't. These days I drink wine because it has less kilojoules than beer; sav blanc, riesling or rosé in summer, shiraz in winter. If it's beer, sometimes I'll buy low carb but still full strength. There is *nothing* quite like that refreshing bitterness on a stinking hot day. Cider is way too sweet for me. Going out for lunch or dinner with friends always included a drink, always. If a restaurant doesn't serve alcohol, which is rare but they do exist, then I don't like that restaurant at all. It just feels wrong to me.

My tastes have changed over the years. When I first started drinking, I drank sweet wine with orange juice. Now I'm at the other end of the spectrum and prefer dry, bitter or even smoky flavours.

Then lockdown happened and I started working from home. And because we couldn't go anywhere, cocktails at home became my new hobby. Especially vodka ones. Delicious cocktail recipes to try out were available on one of the vodka websites, cocktails with raspberry or watermelon, for example. I learned how to make *all* the classics, and anything I had ever tried and liked. Most were quite simple and so tasty: Espresso Martini, Mai Tai, Negroni, Manhattan, etc. Ingredients were easy enough to find usually, or substitutions could be made. For example, I couldn't find orgeat syrup for Mai Tais, but almond flavouring does the trick.

My absolute favourite cocktail is a Key Lime Martini: 45 ml vanilla vodka, 30ml fresh lime juice (half a lime) and 30ml sugar syrup. Shake with ice, and serve in a martini glass with a slice of lemon for a lemon/lime effect. The vanilla adds a divine creaminess. There was no vanilla vodka at Batemans Bay, sadly.

Another favourite of mine is a Purple Rain: 60ml plain vodka and 30ml blue curacao (a fun thing to have in your cupboard). Pour over ice in a tall glass and fill up with cranberry juice. You get a tasty drink with a gorgeous deep purple colour. Serve with a slice of lime for a stunning visual contrast. This one is a healthy drink, because it's mostly fruit juice after all. Unfortunately, I couldn't find any blue curacao at Batemans Bay either, so that one is off the menu too.

Yesterday, late afternoon, I was enjoying an Espresso Martini on my veranda. I'd recently splurged and bought martini glasses in Batemans Bay, which I'm sure *did* improve the taste. Fran walked past on the path below and commented, 'That looks nice!'

I said, 'Would you like one?'

Fran just smiled, replied, 'No thanks,' and kept walking. I watched her slowing down, and then she stopped. She turned around, walked back and said, 'Actually I would like to try one, if you don't mind.'

I jumped up, 'Take a seat!' I was surprised and pleased and to be honest, a bit nervous.

An Espresso Martini the way I make it is a shot of hot coffee (instant unfortunately but it does the job), a shot of Kahlua and a shot of vodka. Shaken (using my drink bottle) with ice and then poured into a martini glass. Ideally decorated with three coffee beans but I didn't have them.

Fran took a sip and smiled broadly.

'It tastes as nice as it looks! How much sugar does it have?'

'I don't know, but only the Kahlua has sugar as far as I know.'

Then we had our first real conversation, I think the alcohol thawed her out a bit.

I asked, 'How long have you been running the cabin park?'

'Ten years with my husband, and fifteen on my own after he died.

'At first this was just an unpowered caravan park, but my husband decided to build cabins instead. We did really well, for a long time, but then the caravan park bought land along the river. It wasn't too bad when it was just caravans there, because it's a different market, you see. But then, they built cabins too, and undercut me! Bastards!

'I'm hanging on though, enough people prefer coming here because of the extra space.'

'And the beach view and the privacy,' I added.

She smiled. 'Soon, I'll start renovating inside the cabins, once the painting's finished. I'm gonna put in new flooring and modern furniture. But I reckon the garden upgrade's made a *huge* difference already. The other thing I'm trying now is having posters put up in Sydney and Canberra.'

I commented, 'Well that's why I'm here, because I saw your poster in Sydney.'

'Oh, well that's good to know!' She seemed genuinely pleased.

'Winter's always quiet,' she went on, 'my best time is summer of course. The market's big enough for the both of us, then.

'Once the renovations are done, I'll charge a bit more,' she confided.

Then she told me about hiring Jake, how he was not so good at admin or cleaning, but had really taken to the gardening.

I asked, 'What do you do when you're not working?'

'Oh, I go to the club for meals sometimes, but I *never* play the pokies. Sometimes I go and visit people, I know everyone in Tomakin! I've got some good friends I've made over the years.'

I learned that the name of the fisherman was Sam.

Fran said her lifestyle suited her down to the ground, all she needed to do was some admin and clean the cabins.

We sat in comfortable silence for a few minutes, then she said, 'I'd better get going. Thanks!'

2005

Very gradually, my relationship with Z began to change. Something shifted, it was like we had turned a corner. I wasn't sure, but thought this probably happened to all relationships as time went on. People start to take each other for granted. It was just little things at first, for example, he started doing things like making himself a cup of coffee and not asking if I wanted one too. The sex was now just all about him.

Sometimes he just didn't answer me if I asked him something. He managed, somehow, to give the impression that what I had said was just too stupid to bother answering. What was I supposed to do about that? Ask if he had heard me? I knew damn well he had heard me. Ask why he didn't answer me? Say, 'Hey! I'm talking to you!'? 'Answer me or I'm leaving!'? I tried all that. Z just laughed at me.

But that wasn't all. He started to criticise me; I did the dishes wrong, he didn't like the way I cooked. One example was mashed potato. My way of making it had always been to add butter and milk and salt and pepper, and leave it a bit chunky, because it had more flavour that way. When Z made mashed potato, it looked like paste, was thin and watery and had no flavour. But my way was simply wrong, according to Z. I tried making it his way, but it was never smooth enough for him. He would sometimes just sigh and scrape it into the bin from his plate.

The days of compliments were definitely over. Z now commented that the clothes I wore didn't suit me. Or they were either too revealing or too dowdy. I could never get it quite right. Sometimes he asked who I was trying to attract? Other times he said why did I dress like Miss Prissy?

My weight increased. Z always insisted I finish my plate even if I already felt full, because it was bad to waste good food. Also, we both liked chocolate, but for me it became an addiction. Family blocks of chocolate became part of our regular food shop. While watching TV after dinner, we would enjoy some chocolate. I can't say no if someone offers me chocolate, or if I know there is some in the cupboard. Z would tease me about this, and say I should have more self-control. I told him it would be better if we didn't buy the family blocks in the first place, but he said he liked chocolate too, why should *he* go without? I should just have self-discipline like him.

Sometimes I did manage to not have chocolate for a few days, but Z would then make sure to enjoy some in front of me. If I was unhappy, which was more and more often, I ate some chocolate because it made me feel good, for a little while at least. Alcohol did that too, of course. And having some alcohol first, made it all the more difficult to not have chocolate. Z didn't put on weight himself because he was larger, a guy, and also because he had joined a gym where he lifted weights. And it was true, he did have more self-discipline.

Z would often say that I was not very bright. I defended myself as best I could, but he was *way* better with words. We would have arguments like all couples do, but he would say things like, 'I never said that,' and would be so confident that I started to doubt myself.

He would say, 'You've got no reason to be upset,' and I would not be sure if I did have a reason or not. I got confused.

There are words for these things now, words like "gaslighting." Twenty years ago though, that word wasn't used, let alone understood. Regarding my relationship with Z, I just knew something was not quite right about it, but found it hard to pin down or explain, even to myself.

Z would blame me if anything went wrong. If he lost his keys, he would say that I must have hidden them. The first time he said that I laughed, thinking he was joking. He was not.

He was often in a bad mood when he got home from work. If he was in a *really* bad mood, he would just look at me and say, out of the blue, 'Don't you start.' Again, the first time he said that, I laughed. Of course I never started anything, but he had the need to take out his bad mood on somebody, and I was there.

One day, Sam gave me a fish. I was walking along the pier, and there was one in his bucket which is usually empty.

I remarked, 'Congratulations!'

He laughed, 'Present for you!'

'Oh thank you! But how can I cook it?' He said in foil on the barbecue, with butter and lemon. I asked what sort of fish it was, he said something that sounded like "mowong." The fish was silver and a bit bigger than my hand.

It was extremely messy to prepare, I had to get the scales off with a blunt knife and the insides out. I'd never actually cleaned a fish before. Luckily, I found some foil in a drawer, and already had butter and lemon. I carried my parcel of fish to the neglected looking barbecue next to the car park, but had no idea how to work it.

Fran was there in the office as usual, she concealed a smile and explained that the barbecue was electric, all I had to do was press the button. I offered her some fish but she declined. Green salad was the perfect side dish to have with it, and it was honestly the most delicious fish I'd ever eaten, so fresh. There was enough there for two meals, I had it cold with rice for lunch the next day.

In the late afternoon, I pulled two beers out of my little fridge and walked back along the pier.

I offered one to Sam, he gave me an enormous smile and said, 'Thank you, I cannot afford but I like!'

He offered me his chair, I said, 'No, no, I'm fine,' and sat down on the pier next to him. We enjoyed our beers, made them last and watched the sunset together in silence. The line he had in the water stayed still, no more fish today.

Beer on the pier at sunset became a random habit for both of us. Gradually, over time, we started to talk.

I asked him, 'Why Tomakin?' He said it was quiet, and had good fish. Because he still had a bit of an accent, I asked him where he was from.

'Vietnam.'

He told me he had set off in a boat from Vietnam with his wife and baby in 1978 after the end of the war, but the boat had capsized and most people drowned, including his family. Sam was one of only two people who survived, fishermen who could swim. They were picked up by the Australian navy.

Sam was accepted as a refugee, learned English and joined the public service in Canberra where he worked for the Department of Statistics. Eventually, he remarried, another widow from Vietnam. They had no children and she died in middle age of cancer. When he retired, he sold his house and bought a boat.

'Always my dream, but I never have enough money before.'

Sam was content living frugally on his pension, supplemented by selling fish to the club. He also had some Super, but that was only used that for emergencies, like the dentist. Most days he took the boat out to sea, but also fished off the pier every day.

'Sunset is best time!'

Sam lived on his boat, sleeping in the cabin. It was comfortable enough, he said, and no one bothered him. The shower block on the beach was his bathroom. Technically, he wasn't supposed to live there, but a blind eye was turned.

I asked him what he did for company.

'I have radio. When I eat, I have seagulls!'

Sometimes he ate at the club and played the Pokies, but not too often. He caught the bus to Batemans Bay for cash and supplies, just like me.

Now and then Sam would fly back to Vietnam to visit relatives, but he had sad memories there and felt more at home in Australia now. There was one relative in Australia, a young cousin, but Sam didn't stay in touch with him because he was into drugs.

I see Sam as a shy, gentle loner with bad memories, but at peace now with his own company. A bit like me really.

He never asked me about myself, which I appreciated.

2006

One day we had an awful, awful argument that I didn't feel we could come back from. Z called me selfish, stupid, a moron, deluded, unhinged.

I said, 'Look in the mirror.' Then I yelled, 'OK, that's it, I'm leaving. I'm not putting up with your shit any longer!' I'd never said anything like that to him before, it took a lot for me to really lose my temper, but I was white hot with rage.

He actually paused. He could see I was serious, that I might actually do it.

And he caved! He pleaded, 'I'm sorry, I love you, I didn't mean it, please don't leave me, I'm begging you, you're all I've got. I don't know what comes over me, I'm so, so sorry.' He actually started crying.

And I fell for it. I couldn't do it, it would have been like kicking a puppy. He said he would see a counsellor about his anger, please give him another chance, he would change.

That's when I should have left. While I was still angry enough and strong enough.

But I gave him another chance. I wanted to believe him, and still wanted our relationship to succeed. Z did see a counsellor, once, but he said they didn't know what they were talking about, so that was the end of that. And nothing changed.

July 2022

Today I decided I really needed to go to a hairdresser, and I chose one I had seen in Batemans Bay. The salon is newish, opposite the Coles in the arcade, so not on the street. A blackboard on the footpath outside advertises, "Hair by Daniel." When I first arrived here, that space had just been an empty shop for lease, but it had obviously been a hairdresser before that, with existing mirrors and chairs etc.

Then one day, there was Daniel. At first, the salon had posters up of young people with brightly coloured hair, tattoos and piercings. That wasn't really the Batemans Bay vibe, so soon enough those posters came down and a price list went up. Prices were about half of what they would be in Melbourne, so I decided to give myself a treat for my upcoming birthday.

The front wall of the salon is completely glass. You can see the two chairs, mostly they are empty but now and then a customer is seated, usually an elderly woman. Occasionally a guy might be in there getting a clipper cut, and once I saw a stressed looking parent with a screaming young child.

There appears to be only one hairdresser, Daniel I presume, who looks to be about my age. He is quite lean, but has impressive arm muscles. When I first saw him, he had spiky, bleached hair but when the posters changed, so did his look. Now he has a neat beard and shorter, styled up hair.

Not having a phone, I couldn't ring to make a booking, but it didn't look like I really needed one. Today before I shopped at Coles, as the salon was empty, I just walked in. Daniel welcomed me, and exclaimed, 'I love your jacket!' as he hung it up (the one with palm trees). We had the usual discussion about what I wanted and I decided to just go with more platinum foils and a cut. My regrowth was about four inches by now, plus my streaks of silver were getting noticeable. I hadn't thought about my hair at all, for months.

Daniel brewed me a good coffee, mixed up the colour and started painting my hair. We got talking and it turned out he was from Melbourne too. He had come here with his partner a few months ago for a change of scenery. Unfortunately, his partner hadn't been able to find work yet so it was a bit tough for them at the moment. I gave him my cover story about being a writer, he seemed slightly impressed.

Then Daniel confided that he was really worried about his cat, which had gone missing. He showed me some photos, the cat was a gorgeous, big, grey and white fluffy thing with a beautiful face and blue eyes. In one photo it was at the top of a tall tree, which was an impressive photo. The cat's name was Luna.

As I was admiring the photo, another customer walked in. She was a large woman in a floral dress who plonked herself down in the other chair.

She said, 'Hi Daniel, just the usual, thanks,' completely ignoring me.

Daniel replied sure, no worries. My foils were completed by now, so he led the woman to the sink, washed her hair and then sat her back down. She had dark curly hair and he efficiently gave her a thorough trim. The woman talked non-stop the whole time about her kids, how they were doing really well in Sydney and how she had a grandchild on the way blah blah blah. It was like a wall of noise, she barely took a breath. Daniel made appropriate noises here and there when he could. Then she changed topic and talked about her old dog, who was on his last legs and had just come home from the vet.

I think Daniel saw an opportunity, so he mentioned his missing cat.

She said, 'It must be hurt or sick and gone away to die. That's what they do.' Daniel dried her hair, she made another appointment and left.

I said, 'Your cat could just be stuck somewhere, sometimes they go into places and can't get back out easily, or maybe it got locked in a garage.'

'I really hope so,' he sighed.

Daniel then trimmed my hair into a shorter bob style, which looked great, even a bit classy. He had just finished the drying when his phone made a noise. A huge smile spread across his face, and he showed me a photo of a guy who actually looked a lot like him, cuddling Luna.

He made a call and had an excited conversation, then told me that their neighbour from across the road had just come over and asked if they had lost a cat? There was one hiding under his house and it wouldn't come out. Daniel's partner (the guy in the photo) had hurried over and sure enough, it was Luna. He had used a can of tuna and managed to entice Luna out, then just carried her home. Luna was thinner, but unharmed. It seemed that she had just been too scared to come out, probably because the neighbour owned a large bulldog.

Daniel said, 'You were right! Let's have a glass of bubbles to celebrate!' I was happy to accept and said I was really pleased for them. He nipped across to Coles and came back with some prosecco. We then joyfully polished off the whole bottle. Daniel closed up early and went home to be with his cat.

I did my shopping and also bought some prosecco, to have by myself at home to celebrate Luna's homecoming.

On the bus ride back to Tomakin, I thought about the woman and what she had said to Daniel about the cat, and why. Maybe that was her lived experience, or what she truly believed must have happened. Maybe she thought she needed to prepare Daniel for the worst. But, then again, it could just be schadenfreude, "joy in another person's sorrow."

Z was like that too. He liked imagining the worst possible scenario, then making sure the other person was aware of it. He was then disappointed if the story or situation was actually resolved in a good way.

One time, I asked him why he thought like that, he replied because that had been his experience in life. I remember saying I didn't want to think like that, he said he couldn't help it.

A classic example was when I applied for a promotion at my work. A supervisory vacancy had come up and I thought I had at least a chance. First a written application was required, followed by an interview panel. A handful of my colleagues had also decided to apply. Z was positive I wouldn't get the job, because these things were always rigged, he said.

My written application took a couple of hours to complete, I did my absolute best, but didn't end up scoring an interview. Feedback was given to me that my application was of a high standard, but other applicants were more experienced. I was also told not to be discouraged and try again, next time it might be me. This sounded reasonable to me, until I got home and told Z.

He said, almost gleefully, 'See, I told you you wouldn't get it, they already know who they want before they advertise.'

'I was told it might be me next time.'

He just scoffed, 'Dream on.'

Saturday 9 July 2022 4.00 pm

I've just realised that today was my birthday, and it just so happens that I didn't speak to another soul.

Keeping track of days and dates without a phone is difficult. I try and catch it on TV if possible and I know it's a Wednesday if the weatherman is wearing a vest. Sometimes I'll buy a newspaper in Batemans Bay which of course has the date, or I'll notice that the café is closed because it's a Sunday. The cabin park is the same every day, except that Jake isn't here on weekends.

Some days I just don't end up speaking to anyone at all, not by choice, but by circumstance. If I'm in Tomakin, visiting the café is the only time I speak to anyone, that is, if I don't run into Fran or Jake, or have a beer with Sam.

I knew my birthday was looming. Today I had the thought that I really should sit down and work it out. So I drew up a calendar and it turns out that today's the day. And today just happened to be one of the days when I didn't talk to anyone. Never mind. It's not really a problem. But tonight I'm going to have a party for one, a couple of cocktails and chips and chocolate. No actual healthy meal for a change.

I feel a bit down, I suppose, being completely alone on my birthday. But then again, I feel safe and strong and in control. There have been worse birthdays than this.

Z was an extremely bad, though seemingly lucky driver. He always drove, because it was his car, but he would speed, not indicate, change lanes suddenly, drive too close behind people.

Consequently, I became a nervous passenger. Sometimes I couldn't help jumping, or shouting, 'Look out!' Z would get angry with me, because I "didn't trust him." He would then drive even more aggressively.

Often my job was to navigate, which I found difficult. This was all before Google Maps existed so I had to use a Melways which was not up to date. I did my best but sometimes we would end up lost. It always had to be my fault, even if I knew it wasn't. Z complained that I was hopeless with maps, like all women. He would never stoop to asking anyone on the street for directions, so sometimes we would just drive around lost, for ages.

Another absurd thing with Z was that if we were in a crowded car park and had to wait for a spot, he would get really annoyed that the other driver was "being an arsehole and making me wait." But, if someone was waiting for *us* to leave a car spot, Z would deliberately take as long as possible and again call the other driver an arsehole for being impatient.

One year, for my birthday, we decided to go on an extended day trip by car to the snow. This was my idea, something I'd always wanted to do, and Z also liked the idea, for a change. I planned our route to be as scenic as possible, and was really looking forward to doing something completely different for my birthday.

We rose early, ate a quick breakfast and drove out of the city on deserted streets while it was still dark. Soon enough, we were driving into a glorious sunrise. It was actually a beautiful drive through lush green bushland on narrow curvy roads. We drove through small, sleepy country towns, past empty green paddocks and solitary farmhouses. Quite a few bridges over fast flowing rivers had to be crossed on our journey up to the mountains. It was a clear day, the sun became so bright that we needed to wear sunglasses. The air was brittle and frosty, you could smell the snow in the air.

Mid-morning, we stopped for coffee and delicious fresh pastries at a small bakery, in a country town I don't remember the name of. The bakery was old, and done up like a saloon in an old western, you walked through those swinging gates to get in. Both of us enjoyed the quirkiness of that place.

After another couple of hours, we reached snow country. Big signs were up here and there, stating, "CHAINS MUST BE FITTED ON ALL CARS!" Z didn't agree with that, he said it was only necessary if there was black ice. I became quite worried because he always drove too fast and could be quite careless sometimes.

We had to stop for petrol and I actually stood up to him for once, said I wasn't going any further unless we got some chains.

'Well I'm not getting chains. So you want us to turn around and go back home after driving all this way?'

I said no, of course not, I just thought we should obey the signs. I said we might get a fine. I didn't dare say I just wanted to be safe.

Z was furious, but I stood my ground.

He finally conceded, 'OK, but I'm only doing this because it's your birthday, and you're paying for the chains.' I was surprised, and relieved, Z *never* usually backed down or changed his mind. Chains were fitted onto the car at the next garage.

Driving on, soon we reached some actual snow, and parked in a large busy car park. I noticed that there were chains on *all* the other cars, most of which were SUVs. Many families with excited kids were there, all nationalities. Some of the cars had cute little snowmen on their bonnets, and a bunch of kids were making a huge snowman a bit further up the mountain.

The rest of the day was ruined for me as Z was in a glowering bad mood. We followed a path to a lookout and got cold and wet, neither of us had proper clothes or boots for the snow. We could have hired some, but by then it was too late. Toboggans were also available for hire, but Z didn't feel like it.

A fancy, expensive restaurant was nearby which looked like a chalet in Switzerland. Luckily, we managed to snag a table near the window for lunch. Z spent the whole time gazing at the view and totally ignoring me as we ate. I tried my best to enjoy the meal, but it was difficult.

During the long drive back, there was complete silence. For hours and hours. All I could do was sit there, trapped in Z's bad mood. I knew that there was nothing I could say or do to change anything. All I could do was endure, and think. I realised that this car trip was a metaphor for our relationship; it had started off full of promise, some of it was enjoyable, but then it became more and more unpleasant. It was impossible to get out of a moving car that Z was in control of.

When we finally returned to the city, it was dark again. Z just parked the car without a word. He ate by himself, had a shower and went to bed. I'd managed up until then to keep it together, but I just sat there and wept.

So that was my birthday.

Z apologised for his behaviour the next day, said he was just in a bad mood because of the chains. He acknowledged that he had ruined my birthday and said he was truly sorry. In a surprise move, he then presented me with a stunning silver and jade necklace as a belated birthday present. I accepted his apology, what else could I do?

Z was able to convince me that it was no big deal, everyone had bad days now and then, it was just part of being in a relationship. He was especially nice to me for a few days, it was almost like it had been in the early days of our relationship. He knew exactly how to unbalance me, to keep me sweet. Then he went back to being his normal, grumpy self.

Sunday 10 July 2022

It was a still, overcast day in Tomakin. The beach was deserted, as it often is for my walk. Clouds were looking a bit menacing, but they didn't change and were stationary, like an oil painting of an impending storm.

A small silver boat was out at sea, it seemed to be keeping pace with me somehow, which was strange. But I don't know anything about boats and how they move.

This boat was much smaller than Sam's, it was just a tinnie. A man was sitting in the boat, dressed in black, wearing a hoodie. He was completely still, his hand on the tiller, facing straight ahead. It was too far to make out his face at that distance. The engine noise was a monotonous drone, there was no other sound.

I reached the end of the bay and stopped, the boat stopped too. It just sat there, gently bobbing on the waves.

Suddenly, I felt scared. I started to run back along the beach, and the boat turned and started coming towards me. The engine noise was louder now, and the boat picked up speed.

It became hard to run, the sand was now closing over my shoes like quicksand. I began to sink. I looked out to sea, and the boat was headed straight at me. Now I could recognise the man.

It was Z. His pale blue eyes were expressionless, mesmerising, I couldn't look away. The boat came closer and closer to shore.

Finally it hit the sand and the engine stopped abruptly. Now the silence was complete.

Z stepped out of the boat carefully, and took his time walking towards me.

I struggled desperately in the quicksand, screaming. Now it was like my feet were encased in concrete. Z slowly reached out towards me and I woke just before he touched me.

Sweat covered me, I think I actually *had* been screaming. The bedclothes were tangled around my legs. It took me a few minutes to calm down and get my breath back.

I managed to get up shakily, make a coffee, and climb back into bed. It was very early in the morning.

It must have been the alcohol and lack of solid food last night. Alcohol really doesn't do me any favours, sometimes. I've been sleeping quite well at Tomakin and don't dream, or if I do, I don't remember. This nightmare was vivid, extremely realistic, one of the worst I've ever experienced.

I don't believe for a moment that dreams foretell the future. As far as I know, they are just visualisations of what is currently in your mind. I've managed not to think about Z much on a conscious level since I've been here in Tomakin. But I do know he is out there somewhere, thinking about me, which is chilling. In fact, he's probably still looking for me, I know how obsessive and determined he is. I imagine him combing through hours and hours of CCTV, he would have easily been able to find out I'd withdrawn $10,000.

All I can really do is hope that he can't find me.

Monday 11 July 2022

This morning, I wanted to ask Fran about booking for another month so I headed to the office, about 10.00 am. Unusually, the door was still locked, Reception hours were always nine to five. There was no response to my knock, so I started walking back to my cabin. But I felt uneasy, the office was *always* open at this time, either Fran or Jake were there, or at least the door was open and you could press the buzzer.

I turned around and headed back to the office. Just then, Jake appeared, coming in the gate. I asked him, he said he didn't know. We both knocked on the door again, more loudly this time.

He commented, 'Her car's here, maybe she's still asleep?'

I had a bad feeling. 'Do you have a key?'

'No, there's only one master key and it's always kept in the office.'

I said ring her, he did and we could hear her phone ringing inside. Jake followed me around to the back, and peered in through a gap in the curtains.

In a relieved voice, he said, 'See? It's okay, she's still asleep.'

He stepped back and I looked in, she was lying in bed, her back to the window, quite still. I banged loudly on the window, she didn't stir.

'Call an ambulance!' I shouted.
'What?'

'Just give me your fucking phone!'

The ambulance arrived in about 20 minutes, sirens blaring. Two ambulance officers, both young men, forced open the front door, which we had not been game to do, and rushed inside. Jake and I followed. I'd never been in the back part before, I noticed leather furniture and a Persian rug. The ambulance officers asked us to wait outside, Jake was wide eyed and started pacing up and down. A few nearby locals, who must have heard the ambulance, came into the carpark and just stared.

After about ten minutes, one of the ambulance officers came outside and told us Fran was okay, but weak; she'd gone into a diabetic coma. He asked us some questions, most of which we didn't know the answer to, like her age, when she had last eaten etc.

He did say, 'It's a good thing you rang us when you did!' He told us they were just going to take her to hospital to run some tests, and make sure she was OK. Fran was wheeled out to the ambulance on a stretcher, the relieved crowd gave her an encouraging cheer. She managed a weak smile and wave.

Jake was able to fix the door, and was happy for me to sit in the office that day. He hung around though, doing some painting on Cabin 1. I fetched a book from my cabin and spent most of the day reading. No-one came in to the office at all. There was one phone call, which I managed to deal with, about prices for cabins. Just before I closed up for the day, I rang the hospital and was advised that Fran was OK and on her way home. I informed Jake, he was relieved and rushed home to tell his mum.

Staying in the closed office, I sat there reading until Fran arrived, in a taxi this time. She took her time getting out of the taxi, and I helped her slowly up the stairs. It was a shock to see how different she looked, pale, weak and shrunken somehow. Actually, she looked frail.

Sitting back in her chair, Fran spoke quietly, 'So you saved my life.'

I said anyone else would have done the same, she retorted, 'Apparently not Jake!' I just shrugged, I wasn't going to defend him.

'I didn't know you were diabetic, but my grandmother was, so I know all about it,' I explained.

Fran replied, 'I don't tell people. I'm very careful usually, just this once I must have forgotten to take my tablets. I'm an idiot!'

She needed to get to bed, I asked if there was anything I could do? She gave me a lovely smile and said, 'No, but thank you.'

And then we were friends.

2005

I used to have an international pen pal, we'd been writing to each other ever since we were in High School, starting at the age of about thirteen. My pen pal lived in Scotland and her name was Chris Coffey. We'd write about the music we liked, school, our friends, family, the usual teenage girl stuff. Chris was one of a large family, she had an older brother who sounded cute, so I was always asking about him. She liked different music to me, she liked the Beatles, Michael Jackson. I liked AC/DC, the Angels, Midnight Oil. Most of the bands I liked were Australian, and she'd never heard of them. I was going to send her a CD of some music, but never actually got around to it.

Chris and I told each other everything, how our parents were overprotective, crushes we had at school. Both of us went through a stage of being obsessed with our weight, trying new diets like the Atkins diet. We tried it together, and gave up on it together.

As we moved into our twenties, we wrote less, probably every few months. Chris was still living at home when I moved out into my first share house, she had a steady boyfriend by then and was engaged.

When I moved in with Z, I sent Chris my new address, but didn't get any more letters from her. I thought maybe she hadn't got the new address for some reason, so I sent it again, but got nothing back. This made me a bit sad, I *had* thought we would always write to each other, but accepted that she must have moved on with her life.

When I had been living with Z for a few years, one day I ran into a neighbour at the gate. We lived in apartment eight upstairs, she was in apartment three downstairs. She handed me a letter which she said had been put into her mailbox by mistake (the eight did sort of look like a three). The writing looked familiar, on the back of the letter was written the name Chris Elwood.

Taking the letter inside, I was excited and intrigued. Z happened to be out shopping at that time, so I sat down with a coffee and read the following:

"Dear Pen Pal,

This will be the very last time I write to you. I'm sorry, but it's hard writing and not getting any reply, for years. I've kept doing it anyway, just hoping for at least one letter back. I'm sure I've got your address correct, you did send it to me twice! Maybe you've moved again?

I hope you are going well with Z. As you can see from my name, I am married now and we have just moved into our own house. I won't send you my new address, because then I will be disappointed yet again if you don't write.

If you just got bored or fed up with writing to me, please just say so. I'll understand! Just send one final letter. Please! At least then I'll know. Otherwise I'll keep imagining the worst, that something might have gone wrong in your life.

Anyway, hope you are OK, and that your life is going well. It was great getting to know you through your letters. I'm keeping them in a box, for now. I do treasure them. I'm really hoping I've just been writing to the wrong address.

Goodbye.
Chris."

I read it through a few times and then put the letter down, my coffee forgotten and cold. So she *had* been writing. For years. It didn't make any sense, why hadn't I been getting her letters then?

Z knew about Chris. I had told him how much had I enjoyed getting her letters, how we told each other everything. Then how I was sad that she seemed to have stopped writing. He said, oh well, everyone lets you down sooner or later, she must have got bored.

Z always brought in the mail, because he said sometimes there were spiders in the letterbox so he would do it.

I thought long and hard about confronting him. He would have denied it, why on earth would he hide or destroy letters? I knew the words he would say, the tone he would use, how he would turn it around to *me* unjustly accusing *him* of doing something he would never do.

At first, I was keen to write back to Chris straight away. I still knew her old address which was her parent's address. But how could I explain what had gone wrong? The thought filled me with shame. Maybe I could just say I *had* given her the wrong address. But that didn't make any sense, how could I explain getting *this* letter? And how would I get future letters? Could I tell Chris to write to Flat 3 and ask the neighbour to keep the letters for me? Should I get a postal address and keep it secret from Z? None of these options seemed plausible, and anyway, they all needed me to explain about Z which I couldn't bring myself to do.

So in the end, after a lot of agonising, I didn't write back. I felt really guilty and sorry for Chris, I just hoped she would just think she had been writing to the wrong address, as she said in her letter. And I thought that maybe one day, I *would* write and explain.

Why didn't Z give me the letters? Did he think Chris was male? Or was it just to stop me having someone to talk to about him? The only conclusion I could really come up with was that he wanted to make my world smaller, one person at a time.

Many years later, when Z was safely behind bars and a bit out of mind, I did write to Chris care of her parent's address. Waiting anxiously for a reply, I understood how she must have felt. But eventually my letter came back, marked "RETURN TO SENDER."

Sunday, middle of July 2022

Today, as I was walking past Reception, I noticed that it was closed and a handwritten sign was stuck a bit crookedly to the window with sticky tape. Curious, I went closer and read "SORRY, OFFICE CLOSED FROM 10.00 TO 2.00 DUE TO FUNERAL."

A bit after two o'clock, I went back. Fran was just opening up and ripping the sign off the window. She was wearing a black dress. I'd never seen her in a dress before, it was just plain, and she also had on a knitted black cardigan and black shoes with a slight heel. She looked quite different, even a bit elegant. Black suited her.

She told me to come in for a cuppa.

'I'm having tea, I suppose you want coffee?' The teapot she brought out was old fashioned with a rose design, and had a matching cup. My coffee came in a mug with a goldfish on it.

I asked who had died, she said, 'Old Annie.' I didn't know who that was until Fran described her and then I *did* know, although I hadn't known her name.

I had seen Annie a few times, she was a very old lady who had wild white hair, and wore old lady dresses and gumboots. Annie wheeled a shopping cart, which she used like a walker, around the streets. Usually there was a cat in a basket in the cart. The cat was black and looked quite old, it had a skinny body which made its head look large.

'Nice cat!' I had exclaimed the first time I had come across her.

Annie had squinted at me, 'Her name is Smoocher.'

I asked how old Smoocher was, the answer was eighteen. I asked if I could pat the cat, she replied, 'Sure, but be gentle.' Smoocher's fur was very soft, she had beautiful golden eyes (like the tiger), and a sweet face. She purred up at me.

I saw Annie and Smoocher around now and then, but after a while, I noticed there was no basket in the cart. I had to ask.

'Gone, in her sleep. Me next!' Annie had cackled. That had been a few weeks ago.

Fran told me that the neighbours had noticed mail piling up at Annie's house. The door wasn't locked (few were in Tomakin) and they had found Annie in her bed. She'd been dead about a week, natural causes.

I mused, 'That's not a bad way to go,' and Fran agreed.

She told me the neighbours had found a beautifully tended, tiny grave in Annie's backyard, freshly planted with flowers and with a small sign on it saying "SMOOCHER."

Fran said that the funeral was quite large, everyone had known Annie. She'd retired in Tomakin with her husband years ago, they had lived a quiet, almost secluded life until he had died. There were no kids as far as Fran knew. Then Annie had started taking her cat for walks in the shopping cart. She had done that for years, starting when the cat was a kitten.

Fran offered me another coffee which I declined. She poured herself another cup of tea, and then told me a story about something that had happened at the cabin park around seven years ago.

'A young couple checked in for the weekend. They were *really* young, the guy had his driver's licence, but only just. They were from a very small town, inland from here.

'The guy was confident, good looking. The girl was really shy, she hid her face behind her long blond hair. They held hands *all* the time.

'I saw them walking to the club at dinner time, all dressed up. They were such a good looking couple! She was in a black lacy dress, with high heels that she could only just walk in, and he was in a nice shirt. Then later on, I saw them sitting on their veranda with a slab of beer.'

Fran poured herself yet another cup of tea, this one looked very dark. Taking a sip, she grimaced and put the cup down again.

She continued on with her tale.

'Very early the next morning, which was Sunday, I saw the girl running to their car. She had tears pouring down her face and stalled the car a few times before she drove off. *I* thought they must have had a fight. I hoped she'd come back and that they'd patch it up. But she didn't.

'Much later that day, I noticed that the curtains were still drawn in their cabin, so I thought he must have left too.

'Anyway, checkout time came on Monday, and I went to clean the cabin. The door was locked so I had to use the master key. The guy was still there, lying in the bed. He was cold, dead and there was a needle and drug stuff on the table.'

'That must have been so awful for you!'

'Yeah, I was really sad. I called the police and ambulance, and they told me that he actually hadn't been dead that long, only a few hours. I still feel guilty. If *only* I'd checked earlier, maybe he could have been saved!'

I said, 'Yeah, but you had no reason to think anything was wrong.'

'Well, the curtains were still drawn, *that* was unusual.

'The police got his address from his driver's licence, and had to go and tell his family. And his family told them who the girl was. She lived in the same street, they were childhood sweethearts!

'I heard later that she'd locked herself in her bedroom. Her parents just thought she'd had a fight with her boyfriend, and were leaving her alone, they thought she'd come out when she was good and ready. The police didn't force her out of her room, they got a social worker to persuade her to come out.

'The girl told them she didn't know where the drugs were from, her boyfriend had got them. It was their first time trying heroin, they really didn't know what they were doing. He injected her first, and then himself. She remembered feeling dizzy and lying down. Next thing it was morning, and she couldn't wake him up. She'd just panicked and fled. She was only sixteen.

'Everyone was so sad, both here in Tomakin, and in their home town. No-one blamed the girl. For a while, people left flowers outside the cabin here, and some people wanted a plaque. But I said no, I thought it might spook guests.'

'Which cabin was it?' I asked.

'I'd rather not tell you.'

'What happened to the girl?'

'I don't know, but I heard the family moved out of that town.'

We sat in silence for a few minutes. Then I suggested, 'Tell you what, let's have a drink to toast Annie.' I offered to make Espresso Martinis but Fran said no, she had a better idea.

After clearing away the teapot and cups, she carefully carried in an antique looking lacquer tray on which were two fine cut crystal glasses, a small bucket of ice, a jug of water and a bottle of Dimple Scotch. I'd never tried Dimple before, Fran said she kept it for special occasions only.

We both chose to have it with ice. Our first drink was to Annie, our second to the young guy. Our third drink was to the young girl. We had yet another glass, and this time drank to, 'A good death!'

We started laughing then, and found we couldn't stop.

Late July 2022

My watch stopped. As I didn't have a phone, I really needed my watch to tell the time if I was out, waiting for a bus for example. Fran told me there was a shoe repairer in Batemans Bay who also did watch batteries, and told me where the shop was. I took the bus the next day.

Finding the shop, I was disappointed to see the metal grill was down. A printed sign was neatly pinned to it, "BACK IN HALF AN HOUR."

So I bought an ice cream, delicious lime gelati this time, and sat on a bench facing the river. After what I estimated to be more than half an hour, I went back. Unfortunately, the shop was still closed. As I was turning away, a guy appeared, unlocked the grille and pushed it up. He was in his twenties, large with a bushy beard. He seemed shy. I asked if he could fix my watch.

'Sure, if it's just the battery. I can send it away if it needs more than that, but I'll let you know.'

He got some tiny tools out and skilfully pried open the back of my watch. While he was working, I looked around his tiny shop. Shoes and boots were neatly sitting in pigeon holes waiting to be picked up, he also did keys and sold torches. Picking up a small red torch on a keyring, I saw that if you pulled it out it became a tiny lamp. I thought that was really clever, and a torch might come in handy.

The guy gave me my watch back and confirmed it was just the battery. I bought the little torch as well, which pleased him. The bill was surprisingly low.

I exclaimed, 'You do such a great job here!' and he smiled shyly.

Every time I walked past his shop after that, I said hi. He always smiled back at me. I wished I had shoes to get fixed as well, to give him more business, but I really didn't.

This guy was about the same age as Jake, but had a much nicer personality. I thought there was something a bit off about Jake.

After getting my watch fixed, I took the opportunity to hunt through Batemans Bay for some warmer clothes. Winter in Tomakin is not as cold as winter in Melbourne, if you just go by temperature. But then again, I am not in a warm apartment with central heating here, like I was in Melbourne. The cold air seeps into my cabin through the thin walls, and it doesn't help that I am sitting still most of the time. Some days the cold is almost unbearable.

There *are* clothing stores in Batemans Bay, but they mostly have swimwear and summer clothes. Kmart also didn't have the sort of stuff I needed.

The two Op Shops; a Salvos and a Vinnies brought me more luck. I managed to find a thick woollen ski jumper in red, grey and white, which fitted me perfectly and felt wonderful, like a warm hug. Then I found a shiny black parka which had a hood with fake fur around it. The parka was a bit big for me, but would definitely do the job. The best thing I found, though, was a long, thick, hand-knitted stripy scarf just like the one Tom Baker wears in *Dr Who*. I love it.

My final purchase was from the camping store, where I found gum boots and knitted gloves. So now I felt prepared, whatever the weather threw at me.

I wear the jumper and sometimes the parka when I am writing in the cabin, but I had to cut the fingers off the gloves so that I could use a pen properly.

Going out in the rain for my beach walk could be really unpleasant though, even if I *was* wearing the parka, scarf and gumboots. If the rain was strong and angled, it would feel like needles were hitting my face. If there was a storm with strong winds, I would actually get blown around. So on days like that, I just stay in, shivering. Hot drinks keep my hands warm, I've rediscovered Irish coffee. Sometimes I just go to bed and read. I even write in bed, in my gloves.

I understand now why very few people come here in winter.

2005

I would never know what could make Z angry. His anger was cold, and he could easily stay angry for a week. I would try and stay angry as well, but my anger could only last a few hours at the most. Sometimes we would have an argument in bed, and then he would just roll over and start snoring. I wouldn't be able to get to sleep myself because I was still angry and stirred up, it was *so* annoying.

Z liked to provoke me and make me lose my temper, that was a win for him. He always maintained that it was fine to yell and let off steam, that it's not healthy to keep things bottled up. His parents had argued all the time, he said, it was completely normal.

But I knew it didn't have to be that way. That was not my childhood. Sure, my parents disagreed about things but I never actually heard them argue, let alone scream at each other. They just discussed things and worked them out, compromised. So I didn't grow up with anger, and I hated it, it really upset me, made me feel sick.

The silent treatment is ridiculous. But it's extremely effective.

One time Z didn't speak to me for three days, I didn't know why. It drove me crazy. I kept guessing what I might have done to "upset" him.

'Please tell me what's wrong?' I pleaded. He ignored me.

By the third day, it became unbearable, I was an emotional wreck. I yelled at him, I cried.

Finally, he admitted he had been conducting an experiment. He just wanted to see how long it took to make me cry. He promised he wouldn't do it again, and hugged me like nothing was wrong.

I was angry, but also tremendously relieved, and just wanted to forget it had ever happened.

When people ask someone, why didn't you just leave, the answer is actually quite simple. It's because it doesn't occur to you that it's an option you can take. Because they have made you think that way.

They undermine your strength and confidence, they feed your insecurity. You begin to doubt your own judgement, maybe you *are* overreacting. Z liked to say to me that I had always had everything handed to me on a platter, I needed to understand what the real world was like.

The other person isolates you so that you have no-one to talk to or ask advice of. By this time, I had no friends left, no family.

They convince you that *they* are your family and always will be. That you are meant to be together, forever. Slowly but surely their narrative takes over.

I began to accept that this was my life. In my parent's generation it was more normal for the woman to be subservient, the man to be the boss and make all the decisions. That was my only model for a relationship. Although in my case, my parents respected and treated each other well.

And was it really so bad? I actually didn't know any more. It was just my life now.

Probably July 2022

Sometimes when I walk past the club at Tomakin, I really wish I could go inside, have a drink, talk to people. At Batemans Bay too, walking past the restaurants and seeing tables of people having a good time, I wish I also had friends to go out with.

I am always at a table by myself, but what I like to do, whenever possible, is to eavesdrop. It's the next best thing to sitting with someone, and I forget all about feeling lonely. I'm discreet of course. Sometimes I hear interesting, entertaining things, and it's like I'm getting a free show.

Today, I was at the Tomakin café sitting at my usual table for one, enjoying the mild weather, a long black coffee and a cookie. One other table there was occupied, a middle aged man and woman having a meal.

An elderly couple came in with a young boy who was about six or seven years old. The boy was young enough to still be a bit cute, but old enough to be strong willed. I guessed the elderly couple were his grandparents, they looked a bit familiar to me. I'm sure they were locals who lived nearby.

The grandmother asked the boy where he wanted to sit, the grandfather suggested, 'Let's sit here in the shade.'

But the boy said, in a loud and surprisingly commanding voice, 'No, I want to sit *there*,' and pointed to a table immediately next to the man and woman eating. So that's where they sat. The man and woman had to move their chairs in a bit.

The grandmother asked the boy what flavour milkshake he wanted, and he said, 'Banana!'

She smiled, 'Coming right up!' and headed inside to order.

The grandfather's phone rang then, and he started chatting.

'Who's that?' the boy demanded.

The grandfather ignored him, the boy started kicking the table leg.

After a couple of minutes, the grandmother came out, and the grandfather finished up his call. She sat down and told the boy, 'Sorry, they don't have banana so I got you chocolate instead.'

The boy frowned, folded his arms, and said, 'I want BANANA!'

Looking stricken, the grandmother replied, 'I'm sorry, love, but they don't have it. Don't you want chocolate? Everyone likes chocolate!'

'I HATE chocolate. I ONLY like BANANA!'

The grandfather said, 'Don't worry, I'll have it then. Problem solved!' I smiled to myself.

The boy started wailing, 'I want to go home, I'm so bored here. Why don't you have a PlayStation like my other Nan and Pop?' He took a deep breath. 'And why did we have to come to this stupid café? I HATE it here!'

The grandmother, looking really embarrassed by now, explained, 'Well, your Mum asked us to take you out so she could sort out her stuff, it was her idea we come here and get you a milkshake. You liked the idea, remember?'

'I don't care, I want to go home RIGHT NOW!' He was starting to get red in the face.

At that moment, the young waitress appeared carrying a tray containing two cappuccinos and the offending milkshake. She set the tray down at their table with a smile, handed out the coffees, and said, 'This must be for you, young man!' placing the milkshake in front of the boy.

I think all the adults held their breath.

The boy waited a moment, then pushed the milkshake over violently, the waitress jumped back but some of it splashed on her clothes.

The grandmother gasped, 'Oh, I'm so, so sorry, I'll pay for dry cleaning…'

The waitress just laughed, 'Don't worry, these things happen.' She calmly picked up the glass and took it away.

The grandfather commented, 'If I was wearing thongs, I'd smack you with one!' to the boy, who looked shocked.

And then the man at the next table said, 'Here, use mine,' and made like he was going to take his thong off.

The boy stomped off, his grandmother running after him. The grandfather stayed and finished his cappuccino, which he raised in a toast to the man who had offered him the thong.

I chuckled all the way back to the cabin park.

2005

As well as not understanding how share houses worked, Z was no good with our neighbours in the flats. He had no concept of the unwritten rules that exist to enable people to live together, or next to each other. For example, how you just have to accept some situations, even if they annoy you a bit. Z was always complaining to me about something or someone; he seemed to thrive on feeling that someone was doing him wrong. He was big on revenge too, which he took to extremes.

Two young guys moved into the flat immediately next to us. I said hi when they were moving in, we chatted a bit and they told me they were medical students. These guys invited their friends over, a lot, and often had parties with loud music all night long. Z would get fed up and bang on the wall, mostly the music got turned down but not always. Sometimes there was a whiff of marijuana as well. Z was very anti-drugs, me not so much.

As time went on, Z got more and more annoyed. He would bang on the wall if there was any music at all, it didn't have to be loud. I got the feeling there was more music noise now, in response. It was too late to try talking to them, it had gone way too far by now. Anyway, in my experience, asking nicely didn't really work either.

I'd been on the other side of this issue once. I was living in another share house in Fitzroy, where our neighbour had politely knocked on our door one day and asked us to turn our music down because she worked from home and found it hard to concentrate. She invited us to come over and see what it sounded like on her side. One of us went over, and came back saying you could barely hear it. Our music stayed at the same level. I didn't really give it another thought, being young and self-centered at that age. That share house was fairly dysfunctional anyway, and we split up and moved out not long after. So the moral of the story, for me, was that sometimes you just had to wait it out.

And honestly, the music from the next flat wasn't that loud at all.

One day I got home from work and was startled to see a police car pulling out of the driveway. I asked Z if he knew why it was there, he just smiled. Then he told me that the police had raided the flat next door for drugs after an anonymous tip off. About time, he said.

I was shocked. 'But they're medical students!'

'So what?'

'They can't become doctors if they have a drugs conviction!'

Z just shrugged and said, 'Good.'

I asked how *he* knew about the anonymous tip off? He didn't answer.

I don't know if they did get charged, I hoped not, but they moved out not long after that. It did seem that they got the last word. The day after they moved out, Z was furious because he found some excrement in our letter box.

Another time, years later, I came home from work one day to find Z was just sitting there, fuming. He glared at me as I came in.

'What's wrong?' I asked warily.

'Did you see the car?' I replied no.

He ordered, 'Go and take a look!'

Underneath the flats were allocated car spots, but they were not closed in. I had a close look at Z's car, it took me a while, but then I saw a deliberate scratch all along one side of the car. It was deep, and looked like it had been done with a key. I checked the other cars, none of them had any scratches.

Z had called the police, they told him to come in if he wanted to make a report for insurance purposes, but it wasn't really a major incident. Z was outraged that the police didn't "take it more seriously." *He* thought they should come out, take fingerprints etc.

'Who do you think did it?' I asked.

'It *has* to be one of the neighbours!'

'But who? And *why*? Couldn't it just be a random person off the street?'

Z replied, patiently, 'Well, why just *my* car then?'

I thought about it, and then remembered, 'What about the other day on the freeway? When that guy in the ute cut you off and then you drove really close behind him for a while. I did think he was following us later, maybe he followed us home?'

'I never drive really close behind anyone, and anyway he didn't follow us, I would've noticed!'

I just shrugged, 'Well. It must be random then.'

Z insisted, 'No. It's definitely one of our neighbours.'

'But *which* neighbour? And why?'

Z said he had no idea, but it was the only plausible answer. I didn't agree at all and we had a bitter argument where he accused me of always disagreeing with him on principal.

After a tense dinner, I went to bed early. Z stayed up late brooding, and I don't know what time he came to bed.

Next morning, I was woken by loud voices outside. It was still fairly early. Looking out the window, I saw two uniformed policemen standing there, talking to a couple of our neighbours.

I woke Z up, I wanted us to go and see what was up. He didn't. That was a bit strange, usually he would have been eager to find out what was going on.

So I got dressed and went downstairs by myself. It turned out that all the other cars now had scratches on them.

The police came upstairs and talked to Z eventually, he said he thought it must just be some random person off the street, used my words in fact.

It ended there, no culprit was ever found.

Still July 2022

I made a new friend yesterday, a dog I met at the beach. As I was just setting off in the afternoon, a friendly dog bounded up to me. He was really pleased to see me and acted like we'd known each other for years. I've gotten to know some of the Tomakin dogs over time, Smokey the Blue Heeler, Ben the Great Dane, K.C. the Cavalier King Charles Cocker Spaniel, George the Vizsla.

I'd never seen *this* dog before, he seemed young, just a bit older than a puppy. He was unusual looking, I think he was part blue heeler, part red heeler, and partly black and white. He was not too big, a handy size. One of his ears was permanently pricked up and the other ear was permanently folded down. He had a lopsided grin and was extremely friendly without actually jumping on me.

I looked around for an owner but there was no one in sight. The dog had a collar and tag and looked well fed and healthy. I wondered if he was lost?

The dog accompanied me on my walk, he came all the way with me. He ran off exploring now and then but always came back. I decided he *was* lost. When I'd finished my walk I got him to sit and looked at his tag, which was shaped like a bone. Engraved on one side was "FUGLY" and on the other, a mobile phone number. I thought his name was a bit harsh.

I called him to come with me and he responded to his name, although he was reluctant to leave the beach. We walked to the café, he trotted beside me and was careful crossing the road.

At the café I ordered a cappuccino and asked the owner if I could borrow his phone, because I'd found a lost dog.

'Of course!' First he gave me a rope so I could secure Fugly to a tree in the shade, then brought out a bowl of water for him. Fugly had a long, long drink, then settled down for a nap, his chin on his paws.

I sat at the nearest table with my coffee and rang the number on his collar. A female voice answered after one ring.

I said, 'I've found your dog.'

'Thank God!'

Assuring her that he was fine, I then gave her directions to the café. After about five minutes a woman in her thirties rushed in and was ecstatically greeted by Fugly. When he had calmed down, she clipped a lead securely onto his collar and untied the rope.

She said, 'Thank you so much, he ran off before I could put his lead on, I've been looking for him everywhere!' Fugly lay down again and didn't look at all sorry.

The woman then insisted on buying me another coffee and had one herself. She told me her name was Jasmin, and that she and Fugly were staying at the caravan park. They were actually here for a Hen's party and Jasmin was one of the bridesmaids. The bride had grown up in Tomakin but now lived in Sydney. The bride's mother was putting on the party tomorrow at the Club, probably to keep an eye on her daughter, Jasmin thought. There was going to be a meal, drinks, a big cake, maybe a stripper.

Jasmin had never been to Tomakin before, but liked it a lot and Fugly absolutely loved it. I asked her about Fugly.

'I got him from a shelter, no-one wanted him because of his looks! But it was love at first sight for me.

'He's clever, he responds really well to training, but he likes to run off if he can.'

'Did you choose his name?' I needed to know.

'No!' she replied emphatically.

'He picked up the name at the shelter and answers to it, so I didn't bother changing it.'

We finished our coffees, I said I hoped she enjoyed the party and gave Fugly a pat goodbye, he thumped his tail warmly.

Today there were no people *or* dogs on the beach when I set off on my walk at about 3.00 pm. I'd been walking for about twenty minutes when I heard female voices behind me. I turned around and saw a group of five women walking along the beach, some of them not actually walking in a straight line. They were all dressed up and wearing sashes. One woman was wearing a white sash: she had to be the bride. An older woman was wearing a red sash (mother of the bride?) and the other three were wearing hot pink ones (bridesmaids). I recognised Jasmin, in a pink sash and long blue silky dress. The younger women all had high heels in one hand

and a champagne glass in the other. One bridesmaid, not Jasmin, had a bottle of bubbles and was topping up their glasses. I could hear the older woman saying the idea of the walk along the beach was to GET SOBER! No one was listening to her, they were all screeching with laughter and spilling their drinks.

I kept walking, they kept screeching behind me. When I reached the end of the bay and turned around, they were still there. The woman in the white sash was now squatting on the sand near the water. The others had made a half circle around her facing outwards, I assumed she was urinating. I knew what was going to happen next and it did. A large wave came and she toppled over, I couldn't help laughing. The others, except the older woman, all howled with laughter. The bride pulled up her pants and did her best to splash them all. The mother had had enough by now and left. The others were all getting quite wet and luckily for me, also decided to leave. I felt like they would have tried to splash me as well, in a good natured way of course, but they were quite out of control.

I was a bit disappointed not to see Fugly with the women, *he* would have really enjoyed going to the beach with them. I hoped Jasmin would take him later.

As I walked back to the cabin I reflected, a bit sadly, that I had never been a bridesmaid. I suppose I am too much of a loner, not exactly by choice.

Probably August 2022

For the past week or so, to satisfy my curiosity, I've been asking people about the origin of the name "Tomakin."

Fran was certain, 'It's named after the first white man to settle in the area, whose name was Tom Akin.'

The café owner thought it was based on the indigenous word for the area, which is also the origin for the Tomago River's name.

Jake said, 'No idea. Never thought about it!' Why did I bother asking him?

I think the indigenous word option is most likely, although I do like to picture Tom Akin, living in a tent, sitting at his campfire, building a hut and fishing. Like a very early version of Sam.

I've been going to the café most days, mainly for the coffee. The owner is a shy man, of retirement age. He is polite, and knows my coffee orders by now, long black or skinny cappuccino, depending on how I feel. He'll even ask if it's a cappuccino day today. Often, there are different teenagers there to bring out the food or coffee, I think he gives them a chance for some work experience. Now and then he is teaching someone how to use the coffee machine.

No one bothers me there, I feel safe and comfortable.

One day (of many), Z came home in a bad mood. He had a new boss at work, a female a bit younger than him. She was from the U.S. and had new ideas. All of those elements were things he didn't like. Also, she was from outside the bank. Up until then, bosses had worked their way up through the ranks, and knew the job. She was from a public relations firm, chosen mainly because the bank wanted to update their outlook and practises.

So, right from the start, Z was against her. She wanted to learn all about his job, what he actually did. Previously he had been mostly left alone. She didn't like some of his methods because they were more or less illegal.

Every night Z would complain about her and I had to listen. This went on for a few months, then one day when I got home he was already there, drinking heavily. I was wary, asked what had happened.

'I've got the sack!'

'Why? What happened?'

'My new boss bitch! We were having an argument and she just walked off! So I followed her into the female toilets, *just* to finish my point, and that meant instant dismissal! *Can* you believe it!'

Actually, I could. I wondered why she had gone into the toilets; obviously to get away from him. All I could do was sympathise and agree with him, suggest he appeal the decision. I helped him write the appeal, but it was a black and white rule, so that was that.

Z started looking for other work in the same field. He was sure that with all his experience and skill, it would be easy to find another job. But he couldn't. It seemed he was on some sort of blacklist. This really angered him.

Those were dark days, whenever I got home from work, it was like walking into the pit of a live, glowing volcano that could erupt at any minute. I did my best to keep him calm, suggested he look for different work. He tried a stint as a taxi driver, but that didn't suit him, he hated drunk people, would really want to hit them. He also didn't want to work with any women, so that made it almost impossible to find a job.

Money became tight, we didn't go out and just ate basic meals.

Z started having trouble sleeping and spent more and more time online, staying up all night in his cave. I didn't know what he was doing and didn't want to know. Sometimes there were loud noises which would wake me up. I felt it was deliberate.

When I complained he said, 'You sleep too much. It's not good for you.' And it was his place, as he kept reminding me.

I tried to explain, 'Even though I don't do physical work, I need to remember things and make decisions. So I need enough sleep!'

'Well *I* need a job! You just complain all the time, it's all about you! What about me, how *I* feel! Some *woman* has wrecked my career!' he yelled right in my face.

I must have looked scared because he calmed down and then apologised for yelling. He went out and bought me some ear plugs as a "peace offering" but they didn't really work.

Next, Z bought some meditation tapes to try and relax. The voice on them was really annoying to me, monotonous and droning. He would have to have it on loud, so that he could "hear it properly." When I asked if he could please turn it down, just a bit, he blew up again.

So I apologised and tried to get used to it. Looking back, what sort of a person uses meditation tapes to bully someone?

To fill in time, Z started improving his hacking skills. He managed to get into my email accounts, both my work and my private one. All he did, luckily, was just send messages from me to me saying things like, "Hi there, guess who this is?" I don't know if he guessed my password, or found a way of getting around it. The trouble with passwords is that they have to be something that you can remember. If someone knows you really well, in fact knows how to get into your head and is very persistent, they can figure it out, no matter how many times you change it.

One day we were watching the news, and there was a story about how people were being tricked into clicking on legitimate looking links and downloading viruses. People were also losing money to the "Nigerian Prince" bank account scam.

Z just said, 'If anyone is stupid enough to fall for that, they deserve to be scammed.'

I don't know if he actually did anything like that himself, but he was capable of it, I'm sure.

One evening, when I came out of the toilet, Z had my phone and said, 'You got a message. Who's Casey?'

'A girl I work with, we send each other jokes sometimes.'

He said, 'Really? I've never heard of a girl called Casey before.'

'Can I use your computer? I'll show you.'

I brought up our work website, and was able to show him a picture of Casey with her name underneath. He was mollified, somewhat, but wouldn't admit he had been wrong. It was almost funny, it reminded me of an episode of *Happy Days* where Fonzie is trying to say he was wrong but just couldn't physically get the word out.

I started using a PIN to lock my phone, but Z always managed to find out what it was. It was a game for him. He would either watch me when I typed it, or even just guess somehow. No matter what I used, birth dates, postcodes, numbers backwards, he could always manage to work it out.

Early August 2022

Fran knocked on my door a few days ago. She didn't want to come in, but stood on the veranda and told me that she had a booking for a bunch of men. They were a group of friends and were going fishing, they came very year, she said. There were four of them, they had booked the two cabins in the middle which had two single beds. Fran said they would be out fishing most days, and usually ate at the club, but sometimes they would drink and be noisy at night. I thought, great.

Thanking her for the warning, I planned ahead. The fact that Fran had felt the need to warn me made me wary. I felt like it might be best if I stayed out of sight, so I only emerged after the men had gone in the mornings. During the day, I stayed indoors and didn't sit on my veranda. I saw the men in the distance on the pier one day, loading a few eskies onto a fancy big black boat. I could just make out the name of the boat, it was called "MUFF DIVER." Its engine made a huge roar, and the boat moved off very quickly. I noticed Sam's boat wasn't there, I guessed he was avoiding them too.

I could hear the men at night, their loud, unfriendly-sounding laughter. Their music was also loud, heavy metal, and it lasted until the early hours. They did seem to spend most of their time fishing, though. They didn't seem to cook their fish, maybe they just took them home for someone else to cook. I thought of them as guys who fish, not fishermen. Sam is a fisherman.

Jake was pleased they were here, he was happy to have other males to talk to. He told me all about them, they were businessmen from Sydney, trying to catch marlin. They all had shares in the boat. I could see he thought they were to be admired, they were successful, probably rich. I'm sure they would have had attractive, maybe token, wives and girlfriends at home, but this was definitely a male only trip.

One evening, there was a knock on my door. I'd dawn the curtains, but of course my lights were on. It was one of the fishing guys, he wore glasses, they'd probably picked him as being the mildest looking. He invited me to come and have a drink with them, said Jake had told them a writer was staying here, they were interested and wanted to meet me. I silently cursed Jake. The man was polite, but there was an air of entitlement about him that I didn't like. He was one of those "Master of the Universe" types who didn't expect no for an answer.

I had my story ready. I said what a shame, I would love to come and meet them but unfortunately I wasn't well, had some diarrhoea in fact, must have eaten some off fish for dinner.

I clutched my stomach and gasped, 'Oh sorry, here it comes again!'

The man looked a bit disgusted, I slammed the door.

He said, through the door, 'Maybe another time then?' I didn't answer.

I kept my lights off at night after that, used my little torch if necessary. The men left a few days later. Fran was pleased they were gone too, they kept her awake, but she said they always gave her a huge tip.

2006

A girl at work had given me a lipstick that I'd admired on her, as a present. It was a dark colour and seemed to last forever. I started wearing it, Z noticed, of course he did.

He demanded, 'Who are you wearing that for?'

'No one. It's a present, from a female I work with.'

He was sceptical. 'Why on earth would a female give you a present?'

'Because she's a nice person.'

One day I couldn't find the lipstick. I asked Z if he had seen it, he said I must have lost it. I knew damn well I hadn't.

'You threw it out, didn't you?'

He replied, with patient sarcasm, 'You're being paranoid.'

Z had a new idea, that we should have a baby. He thought that would fix things and everything would be wonderful again. I was reluctant, but he just overrode anything I said, he was convinced it was the answer to all our relationship problems. He made me throw my pills away.

But I really didn't want to have a baby with him now. I didn't want to be stuck at home relying on him. I didn't want something to connect us together forever. And he was so jealous already of the time I spent away from him at work, how could he possibly share me with a baby who would need me more and take my attention away from him? The idea really scared me, I felt there would be a real risk for any poor baby.

Also, I didn't want yet another young person in the world growing up and thinking that it was alright to treat someone in a relationship like he treated me, that it was normal. And to then grow up and treat someone else like that, or, to accept being treated like that.

So I went to a different doctor and got more pills, kept them in my desk at work and swallowed them there every day at lunchtime. I got the ones that were just Monday to Friday, so there were none to be taken on weekends.

Finally, Z got another job, and things improved slightly. The job was just data entry at home, he had to copy pages of numbers and lists of stock for a hardware company. It was not well paid and was mindless stuff which bored him but at least it kept him busy and earning some money again. And he got to spend even more time on his beloved computer.

I felt like I could breathe again.

This morning I did a strength exercise class with Fran in the "gym." The gym is actually the garage behind Reception. It contains an exercise bike, some weights in a pyramid stand, a kettle bell, and a TV screen on the wall. This is also the guest laundry, with one washing machine and dryer, which are kept extremely clean. I do my washing there once a week or so, and sometimes run into Fran or Jake doing the sheets and towels. Of course, there is no room for a car in the garage, Fran always just parks in the car park.

Fran had set the gym up for guests to use for free, but no one ever did. Jake used the weights sometimes, and Fran used it every second day for her regular strength exercises. She had been nagging me for a while now to do them with her, she thought I would enjoy it. Fran said strength exercises are essential if you are over 55, or your bones will get weaker and you will become feeble. But you should do them anyway, any age.

So I thought maybe I should give them a try, and also it would stop her going on at me. She had all the exercises on DVD, a friend had copied them for her, so she could follow along on the TV. I actually did enjoy doing the exercises, which were demonstrated by two youngish guys in black shorts, polo shirts, and brightly patterned socks with black runners. There were different options for each exercise, easier or harder and different equipment you could use, proper weights or milk bottles filled with water. The guys were good natured and made quite a few dad-type jokes. One guy mentioned something about an albatross, and the other guy then kept asking questions about albatrosses which the first guy couldn't answer. Some of the exercises were easy, and some surprisingly hard. I could only just lift the kettle bell; Fran is way stronger than me. Anyway, it was sort of fun and I felt good afterwards but as I am not over 55 yet, I think I'll just stick to my daily walks.

Now I'm sitting outside a café in Batemans Bay on the river side, my back to the wall. It's actually a lovely day, a slight warm breeze, not cold at all. I've done my food shopping and am rewarding myself with some very berry pancakes with maple syrup and ice cream. They are delicious but the flies like them too.

I am writing, but also eavesdropping on the three people at the next table, an elderly woman with short grey hair and a young couple. One is probably her child, the other one their partner. All three of them are all a bit dressed up, but I missed hearing if it was a birthday, or some other occasion. The older woman is telling them how she has stopped drinking. She said she sleeps better, has lost weight and doesn't need to go to the toilet in the middle of the night anymore. And she is saving lots of money. Definitely food for thought.

After they leave, I decide to have another coffee. Now I am the only person here at this café.

A walking/cycling track runs alongside the river, people walk in pairs or with a dog, but also on their own. I've walked along it before, just to the highway and back. Sometimes there are pelicans on the light poles. Most people coming the other way smile, or even say hello. It strikes me that I could make a life here, maybe. Get a job, get to know people. I already have some friends here.

Maybe I could try a "real," physical job for a change. There is a job ad in a window for a waiter, and a sign up at the Dry Cleaners. Maybe I could even stop drinking, like the elderly woman. It actually seems possible. Just.

Soon enough, I'll need to make another decision, my rent back in Melbourne will be due. One possibility is to go back to Sydney, briefly, and pay my rent in a big bank branch wearing my wig. But I don't feel I can actually return to Melbourne while Z is there. He knows where I live, for one thing, I'd have to move. And the more time that goes by, the more secure I feel here. But I don't want to worry about it right now, I've still got some time.

I did have another dream about Z though.

I was woken up in the dark by some knocking on my cabin bedroom window. Of course, I just hid under the bedclothes. Why do people in movies or TV shows always get up and open the door?

Then there was knocking on the door as well, and on the other windows. I just froze.

My viewpoint changed somehow, now I was looking down on my cabin from above. The roof was a perfect square and I could see four different Z's doing the knocking and trying to peer in.

At that point I woke up, luckily. It was morning and no one was knocking anywhere. That dream shook me though.

2006

One day, during the time when Z was working from home, something very strange happened.
I was coming home from work, and a removalist truck was standing there at the flats. A young female downstairs neighbour was the one leaving. She was standing there, arms folded, watching the two guys loading the truck.

I said something to her like, 'Leaving already? You've only been here a few months, haven't you?' I was just being friendly and a bit curious.

We hadn't really spoken before but we had always smiled at each other and just said hello if our paths had crossed. This girl seemed quite young to me, maybe in her early twenties, and a bit shy. Her hair was long, dark and shiny, I think her background was Indian. She was usually in office clothes when I saw her, today she was in jeans and a jumper.

She said, 'Can I talk to you for a minute?' She looked quite upset.
'Sure, of course.'

She led me away a bit and then said, 'I just want you to know I am not at all interested in your boyfriend.' I didn't know what to say so I just nodded.

She went on, 'The reason I'm leaving is that he makes me feel unsafe. He invited me out for coffee, said he was lonely stuck at home all day. I said no, I didn't feel right going out with him if you weren't there. He took it really badly, said he wasn't trying anything, was just being friendly. I said, "Well let's all go out, the three of us." He said, "Just forget it." And since then, he's made me feel really uncomfortable.'

I was shocked, and believed her instinctively. I asked, 'What does he do to make you feel uncomfortable?'

She said it was hard to explain but he was always around, would appear unexpectedly and make her jump, walk too close behind her, watch her from his window.

She said, 'See, he's watching us now,' and sure enough, Z was standing at the window in our upstairs flat watching us both. When we looked up, he stepped back quickly. But I did see him.

She went on, 'And that's not all. I started getting anonymous notes in my letterbox, telling me to go back to where I came from. I was born in Melbourne!'

At that point one of the removalist guys came up and said, 'OK, ready to go?'

She replied, 'Yeah, let's get out of here,' and climbed up into the truck with them.

I said, 'Wait, tell me more,' but she just shook her head and said sorry, she had to go.

I slowly and reluctantly climbed the stairs up to our flat. I sort of didn't want to know about this. Z opened the door for me and demanded, 'What did she say?'

'What do you think she said?'

He thought for a moment. 'She was weird. At first she was friendly, then all of a sudden she started avoiding me, turned around if she saw me. I've got no idea why.'

I thought that was a clever answer.

I told him what she had said, and he exclaimed, 'That's just crazy! I wouldn't touch her with a barge pole!'

I asked if he had invited her out for coffee and he hesitated.

Then he said, 'Possibly, but I meant all three of us of course, she must have got it totally wrong!'

I pointed out that she must have broken her lease which would probably have cost her lots of money, and she must have had a really good reason to do that.

Z shrugged. 'Her reason is she's paranoid. She sees things that aren't there, thinks things that aren't true. Has her own twisted view of the world!' It struck me that he could have been describing himself. He added, 'And she has big tickets on herself, she really isn't that attractive.'

I thought she *was* attractive, and had seemed genuinely upset. She didn't seem paranoid to me, she seemed scared. I found Z's version of events extremely unlikely. I thought maybe he had tried his flirting game with her, and it had gone wrong for him this time, she wasn't at all interested and this was his form of revenge, extreme as it was. That actually made much more sense to me.

I really wanted to talk to her some more, but she was gone now.

Middle of August 2022

A few days ago I was sitting in the office having a good coffee with Fran, from her coffee machine. We were chatting about nothing in particular. A big, blue, shiny, brand new looking SUV pull up in the car park, and a middle aged man climbed out. He was well dressed in casual shorts and a polo shirt. To me, he looked like he was probably more used to wearing a suit, his clothes were just too new. The man was tall and balding, in his 50s I would say. He looked around and then came into the office.

He greeted us with a 'Good morning!' We replied with the same in a chorus.

Then he said 'I'm looking for a quiet cabin for myself and my good lady wife for a few days.'

Fran replied, 'Sure, let me show you around.'

She reached behind herself for the master key and led him out. I finished my coffee and discretely tried to see the good lady wife who had stayed in the car, but it had dark tinted windows. After about five minutes Fran and the man came back, he signed the ledger and paid for a week. Fran handed him the keys to Cabin 4. Now I saw the wife, when they both took large suitcases from the car and rolled them to their cabin. She was small, Asian and seemed quite young but it was hard to tell from a distance.

Fran told me, 'He really wanted your cabin, but I said sorry. They're grey nomads, or at least he is and their caravan's being repaired. They didn't like the look of the caravan park, wanted more privacy!'

Even though there were two cabins between us, I could hear them that night and also the next morning. They sounded like a porn movie, by that I mean fake, at least the female noises. They tended to stay inside during the day. I noticed Jake hanging around more than usual.

I didn't see much of the new guests except when they strolled to the club for dinner, always dressed up. One day I did see them walking on the beach holding hands, she looked older close up, but still a lot younger than him. He looked proud and happy. In an unguarded moment, she looked bored. I hoped it was a good enough life for her.

2006

At that stage, I had accepted that my life and future was with Z. Any thoughts I might have once had of leaving seemed like an impossible fever dream by now. For one thing, Z controlled the bank account and all my money.

He reinforced to me often that we belonged together, there was no way we would ever part. He warned me that he wouldn't be able to cope without me.

There were still occasional but very rare good times, which I clung to, and used to try and block out the bad times. There was still some hope, that things would change again for the better. They had before.

I tried to convince myself that I was happier being in a relationship than being alone.

I felt that I was a strong person, that I was strong enough to handle it. Maybe that's part of it, if a woman is strong, do some men feel the need to prove they are stronger?

2007

And then *I* got a new team leader at work. How utterly different a new boss scenario can be.

Z complained, 'Why do you get a new boss you like, and I got one I hated?'

'Maybe the gods like me better.'

He was silent for a moment, and then commented, 'You're right.' He was serious, he actually believed that. It was part of his belief that the world was against him.

My new team leader was named Mark. He was young and keen and full of ideas. I don't think he'd been a manager for long, he had that wide eyed enthusiasm for everything. He started fun competitions for us with chocolate prizes. He would have an individual chat each morning, with each of us. At first we were worried, what had we done wrong? But we quickly got used to it. I, for one, enjoyed the chats which were real attempts to get to know us, not just small talk. Mark was quirky, unconventional. He lived a long way away, caught a ferry to work sometimes instead of driving, and had chooks.

Mark did things quite differently to what we were used to. Instead of sitting in an office for our one-on-one meetings, we would leave the building and go for a walk through the city streets while we were talking. And our monthly team meetings were now held in different city restaurants, and included lunch and one drink if you wanted. These were great, and just for fun, we started giving star reviews out of five for the restaurants. We rated: food, view, chairs (how comfortable), toilets (how clean), talent (the waiters).

But, we would also have a real meeting which was actually more productive than in the office, because people were relaxed and came up with good ideas.

When I got home on meeting days, Z could sense there was something different, he even said, accusingly, 'Why do you seem happy?'

Of course I never went to after work drinks now, but a team dinner was organised and I was determined to go. We could bring partners but I didn't want to. I told Z the dinner was mandatory and only for staff. He didn't believe me. But I went anyway, straight after work. I got changed in the toilets.

The team dinner was fabulous. I "let my hair down," drank and chatted. I didn't flirt, of course not, but I realised that this had been missing in my life. Just a simple, fun night out talking to different people.

When I got home, late and a bit drunk, Z gave me the expected silent treatment. I decided I didn't care.

Group photos had been taken at the dinner and were put on our website under "The Team - Social Events." Of course Z saw these. In one photo, Mark had his arm around me and Casey and we were all laughing.

Z started asking probing questions about Mark, trying to find faults. I didn't normally defend people and disagree with Z, but for some reason, this was different. I just felt like I had to stand up for Mark. I told Z that Mark worked really hard, started so early that he was always first in the carpark, and actually cared about his staff.

Z just scoffed, 'Give me a break, he's a boss, he only cares about results, promotions and how *he* looks to management. And putting his arm around you!'

I exclaimed, 'Don't be ridiculous, that was just for the photo! He's got a girlfriend.'

'So now you think I'm ridiculous? Thanks, that really makes me feel good.'

I apologised, said he had nothing to worry about.

I didn't take it seriously. My mistake.

August 2022

I'm sitting writing in Cabin 5 at the moment, because Jake is painting my cabin. Mine is the last one to be done, although Reception hasn't been done yet either. I'm still sleeping in my cabin, but coming here to write, as that's impossible with Jake peering in the windows.

The only difference between Cabin 5 and my cabin, is the painting on the wall. The one here is a beach umbrella, also abstract. It's in the same style as the one in my cabin, so must be the same artist, I should think. Each painting is in different shades of mostly one colour, my sailboat painting is mostly purple and the beach umbrella painting here is mostly teal. I'll ask Fran about the paintings next time I see her, if I remember that is, but right now I think I'll go for my walk.

So I asked Fran about the paintings, I asked if it was a local artist. She said yes.

Then she said, 'Actually, it's me!' She told me she'd taken up painting when her husband died, she'd done a class and "found her own style." When she had a bunch of them, she'd tried to sell them at the Moruya Market, but had not been able to sell even one. So she just put them in the cabins. She asked me, 'What do you think of them?'

I chose my words as carefully as I could, I didn't want to lie to her. I actually didn't like them much, I thought they were like something a child would do, too simple, not enough detail.

Also, I thought the brushstrokes were too thick and clumsy looking.

'I like the idea, and the different colours.'

She laughed, 'Thank you for being kind. I don't really care if people like them or not, I enjoyed doing them at the time and thought I had come up with an original idea!'

I said 'I don't think Van Gogh sold any of *his* paintings and look what happened there.'

'I'm just way ahead of my time.'

I wonder if Jake has any hobbies, any hidden talents? I doubt it. When he's on a break, he always seems to be looking at his phone, playing games or reading something. He gets quite engrossed sometimes, but always closes it down if anyone comes near. I imagine it's something he probably shouldn't be looking at, like porn, or maybe even the dark web, whatever that actually is.

2007

After the work party, Z started picking me up from work in the car when my shift finished. We had two shifts, "earlys" were 8.00 am to 4.00 pm and "lates" were 10.00 am to 6.00 pm. Z would be waiting outside in the Loading Zone where he wasn't supposed to park, with the engine running. I had to be out the door just after my shift finished. So I started running down the stairs, all eleven floors, instead of waiting for the lift, just in case it was full and I had to wait for the next one. It became very nerve wracking. I tried to time my calls, so that I could finish exactly on time, but the work policy was that we had to let the customer finish in their own time, and sometimes they would go over. So if I was on a call that went over, I would pretend I'd lost the call to make sure I could get out the door. I felt really bad doing that.

Of course I had tried to explain to Z that sometimes calls might go over, he said that they only paid me until the end of the shift and I had every right to leave on time.

Because he was picking me up, it meant that he couldn't complete his data entry work on time. I could see that he was going to lose his job again.

I felt like I was living in a nightmare that was just going to get worse, and there was no way out. In fact, it was like I was living in two worlds. The real world was at work, where everything was normal and people were nice. The other world was a nightmare world, Z's world, where everything I said or did could be wrong, for reasons I could not see.

Z's control tightened. He started doing all the food shopping, he said I wasn't capable of making the right choices. He would tell me when to clean something, although I could never do it well enough, and he would often do it again.

He totally destroyed me. I was just a shell, existing. I felt like I was in a dungeon, there was a small window with light far above me, but I couldn't reach it. I felt doomed. Z was spiralling downwards and he wanted me down there with him.

One day, though, when I came out of work (exactly on time) a young male traffic cop was there, arguing with Z. They both had raised voices and both looked angry. I approached warily, I didn't want to make anything worse.

When Z spotted me he exclaimed, 'See! There she is!'

He told me to get in or we would get a ticket. But the cop gave him a ticket anyway, said only delivery vehicles could park there, the sign was clear.

Z threw the ticket at me and drove home, fuming. It was $192.00.

He growled, 'I'm going to get that cop, he'll be sorry he did that to me!' He often said things like that but never carried out his threats.

When we got home Z said, 'OK, I'm not picking you up any more but you'd better text me if you're going to be late. Or else!'

I assured him I would.

It was a huge relief, I wouldn't have to rush my calls and run down the stairs any more and also, I would get some time to myself on the tram.

But the best thing was that Z would now be able to finish *his* work on time and would hopefully keep his job.

2007

The very next day, as fate would have it, I was two and a half hours late home from work because of an attempted suicide by tram.

I was on lates, it was already dark when I left my office building. My tram was there when I got to the stop, I was relieved because I would be home on time. I got a seat in the front of the tram on the right, next to the window. The tram was maybe half full, after 6.00 pm, the number of passengers always dropped off.

I was just gazing out the window, the tram was picking up speed going downhill, when there was a huge thump and the tram screeched to a halt.

The female driver rushed out of her cab and asked, 'Did you see that? Someone just stepped in front of the tram!'

Luckily I hadn't seen anything. The driver was really upset, I put my hand on her arm. She climbed down the steps and rushed over to the person lying on the road, a bit up the hill. I could just see that it was someone with long hair, and there was the glint of lots of black liquid, which I assumed was blood, on the road near the person's head. It was shockingly real.

The traffic had stopped, other people were there by now leaning over the poor figure on the road.

The tram driver got back into the tram and just said, worriedly, 'He looks in a bad way.'

She climbed back into her cab and used her walkie talkie. An ambulance arrived quite quickly and then we could see paramedics starting to work on the person lying on the road.

The driver came back out of her cab and asked us all, 'Did anyone see what actually happened?'

There was no reply, just some head shakes.

'Sorry folks, this tram has to stay put. You'll all have to walk down the hill to the junction, and wait for a replacement tram. I don't know how long that will take, sorry!'

I was impressed, they seemed to already have procedures in place for this sort of thing, it must happen more often than you would think.

As I was walking, I remembered to send a message to Z that I would be late because of a tram accident, but didn't get a reply. Other passengers were walking and talking quietly, everyone was subdued.

Trams did eventually come, but it was a long wait. When I finally got home, Z was extremely drunk and looked like he had been crying. Our dinner was burnt to smithereens.

I asked, 'Why didn't you turn it off?'

'You didn't say how long you'd be, I thought you could get home any second. It's *your* fault dinner's ruined!'

THEN he said, 'You've been with him, haven't you? The first chance you got, and you took it!'

'What are you talking about? Who?'

'Your wonderful boss!'

I was incredulous. '*What?* It was someone getting hit by a tram! They might be dead!'

'Well, why wasn't it on the news then? I can tell when you're lying, go on, you might as well admit it.'

'I think they don't put it on the news, in case it gives people ideas.' I couldn't believe how Z was carrying on for no reason at all. All I could do was shake my head at him and say, 'You're so completely wrong.'

I'd already seen a potential dead body that day, I didn't feel up to dealing with his shit as well, so I just said I was going to bed and we'd talk in the morning. I got into bed and lay awake though, worried, until he finally came to bed. Pretending to be asleep, I could feel him standing there staring at me. I was scared. I'd never seen him that drunk and upset before, and I thought, at that moment, that he really was capable of anything.

But then he just mumbled something to himself and fell into the bed. He started snoring almost straight away. I felt like I could breathe again.

Eventually, I must have fallen asleep. Waking with a start, I noticed light only just starting to seep in through the curtain, so it was really early.

Z was not in bed, and not anywhere in the apartment, which was actually a huge relief. I felt absolutely shattered, I needed much more sleep. Because I was still on lates, I could have gone back to bed for a couple of hours, but I was really worried about Z.

After a shower, I got dressed and decided to leave home early and walk to work for a change. It would take me about an hour, and I thought I might have breakfast at a café I'd never been to but had always wanted to try, near work. There was plenty of time. But my main reason for leaving early was that I *really* didn't want to be there when Z got home.

I enjoyed my walk through the quiet streets, it was like I had the world almost to myself. Not many people were about, just a few joggers and dog walkers here and there. I chose to walk the long way, through the park and enjoyed the feeling of the tall ancient trees towering over me. As I got closer to the city, traffic became busier and there were more people. I realised that probably quite a lot of people walked to work every day. I thought I might start doing it too, I was feeling really energised and positive, and not as worried about Z as I had been.

Reaching the café, which was quite busy, a yummy smell of coffee and toast was in the air. Queueing up, I ordered a fruit salad, croissant and coffee, and then found a tall chair at the window bench. As I was waiting for the coffee, I realised I'd left my phone at home, next to the bed, switched off and charging. That immediately ruined my mood, I knew Z would be furious with me. He always insisted that I be contactable at all times, "just in case." I'd have to call him from work, explain, apologise. I thought of asking someone in the café if I could use their phone, but decided I shouldn't have to do that, Z could wait till I got to work.

As I got in the lift in my building, I realised that first thing today was my one-on-one with Mark, so I had that to look forward to. After dropping my bag on my chair I walked up to Mark's desk but he wasn't there. This was surprising, he was normally *always* there ready. I waited in case he was in the toilet or something, but he didn't appear.

The guy at the next desk, another team leader, saw me waiting and said Mark wasn't in yet, and no-one had heard from him. This was *very* unusual. Mark always stressed how important it was to call in sick if you were late or not coming in, not just so that your work could be redistributed, but so that people didn't worry about you. The guy said they'd called Mark's girlfriend, and she had said that he'd left for work as usual in the car. We both hoped he was just stuck in traffic, not in an accident.

The team leader told me to just start taking calls for now, so I did. This had all taken some time, so I decided to call Z on my first break.

After about an hour, the lift opened and three uniformed police came in. They looked grim. They were directed to our General Manager Jason's office, he let them in and closed the door. We were all curious as hell. After about ten minutes, the police left and Jason told us all to finish our calls, he had an announcement. He looked pale and upset.

It took a few minutes for all calls to be finished. Then we all crowded around Jason. When there was silence, he informed us he had some terrible news. Mark had been found dead in the carpark under our building, he'd been murdered. It was caught on CCTV, and it seemed like he had been targeted. The police would be back the next day to interview any of us that might have witnessed anything, or had any useful information. But for now, the office was closed and we should go home. I was standing next to Casey, she started crying softly.

I ran into the toilets and was violently sick.

Late August 2022

Today I made a new female friend. She is a woman in her twenties, travelling alone in a campervan. Well not completely alone, she has two small, white, fluffy dogs with her.

When I was doing my walk along the beach, she was ahead of me going the same way with the dogs. She had one of those ball throwing plastic sticks, the dogs were cute in little harnesses in fluoro pink and green. The woman had long, sun-bleached brown hair, and was wearing a colourful flowing dress and white runners. She looked like a bit of a hippy, maybe, but a young one. All three of them were having a fun time, she was walking slowly and throwing balls into the water for them.

Overtaking her, we both said good morning, lovely day. When I reached the end of the bay and turned around, they had gone. I guess the dogs only had short legs, so a long walk wouldn't have suited them.

I decided to have lunch at the café, I didn't do it very often, to save money, but now and then I did splurge. A handful of people were there today, including the woman with her dogs. She was at the next table, and I asked if I could use her pepper as there was none on my table.

We started chatting, I didn't mind because she was a stranger. She told me she was staying at the caravan park, would probably be here for a week. She asked me for suggestions of things to see and do. I came up with the zoo, and the river cruise I had done.

She told me she enjoyed the serenity here, and the dogs were really happy to run on the beach.

I said I hoped she enjoyed her stay and was about to leave, when she said, 'Would you like to come and have a drink with me later at the Caravan Park? I've got some beer. And by the way, I'm not gay, not that there's anything wrong with that!'

'I'd love to. I'll bring cocktails!'

She said, 'Stop it!' which made me laugh. So we made a time, 5.00 pm. She added, 'I'm Holly, by the way.' I gave her my fake name.

Walking back to my cabin, I felt elated because I had a spontaneous social event to go to, woohoo.

I took everything with me to make espresso martinis, because everyone (in my experience) likes them. I even took my martini glasses which I wrapped carefully in a tea towel.

I'd never been inside the Caravan Park before. It was bigger than it looked from the outside, and was neatly landscaped with a mown lawn. I saw the rival cabins, a couple of caravans, but only the one campervan.

Holly had set up two striped canvas chairs and a little card table in front of her van. The table had a white cloth on it, as well as small plates of cheese and biscuits and grapes. There was even a small cut glass vase with some wildflowers in it. The dogs were sleeping nearby in little dog beds, one pink and one green.

She greeted me warmly and suggested, 'Lets have some beer first, and then the cocktail, or *cocktails*, can be dessert.'

'Absolutely!'

'Thanks for coming, it's nice to have another female to talk to! Mostly it's men who wanna have a drink with me, usually truckies or tradies. And because I'm travelling alone, they tend to make assumptions about me.'

I told her about the fishing guys. She couldn't believe the name of their boat! I told her how I was a woman on my own, they were already drunk, and they had just assumed I would be happy to go alone and drink with the four of them in their cabin. I said it annoyed me that we couldn't just say no, not interested. We had to be polite, and have a really good reason to decline any invitation. She totally agreed with me.

I asked how long she had been travelling.

'Since January. I finished my law degree last year, and decided to take a year off and just travel around by myself. I had enough money saved from waitressing and I'd been living with my parents, so I really needed a break! This is actually *their* van. They're happy for me to do what I want, as long as I stay in touch.'

I was curious. 'Do you have your journey all mapped out?'

'Not at all! I just drive and see where I get to. Sometimes I choose places just because of their names. I love the freedom of it, not knowing where I'll be next week. And I've met some lovely people on the road.'

'Are they mostly grey nomads?'

'Yeah, mostly. But I've met younger couples too, and families with kids.

'One grey nomad couple I met were taking five years to travel slowly around Australia, they were seeing and doing everything! They had a *humungous* caravan with a bit that popped out the side. They even had a washing machine! They were wonderful people, really fun and friendly, they went out of their way to be helpful to me.

'Some grey nomads can be a bit socially conservative though, probably just cos they're an older generation. If you're not an elderly heterosexual couple in a caravan, sometimes you feel excluded. I met a couple of female friends travelling together who said some people would assume they were gay, and wouldn't talk to them. There was also a gay male couple I met, who said they found it hard as well, sometimes they even got verbally harassed.

'The worst thing people have said to me is, "Where's your boyfriend? What if your van breaks down?" I just tell them I don't need a boyfriend, and I know as much about fixing my van as most people do, or I'd call someone, like most people do.

'Or they'll ask why I'm travelling alone, do I feel safe? It seems hard for some people to understand that I'm perfectly capable and *choose* to be on my own, with my dogs!'

I just said, 'Good on YOU!'

She accepted my cover story about writing a book, but was more interested in how other people treated me, being a woman on my own, and did I get lonely? I said not really, there were people around to talk to if I felt the need, and my writing kept me occupied.

I thought our situations were similar in some ways, we were both women happy to be on our own. The main difference seemed to be that I was staying put, in fact hiding, and Holly was always moving on. Therefore it was easier for me to make friends who I could talk to if and when I wanted to. That was much harder for her. She used social media a lot, she admitted, but it just wasn't as good as sitting and talking to a real person, like we were doing right now. She also missed parties and other events with people her own age. I was past that, really.

Did I envy her? Not really. It would be nice to see lots of new places, sure, but there was a lot of work involved in travelling like she did. She had a toilet on board, but had to empty it at designated places, had to set up and pack up every few days, and always had to deal with new people.

We'd finished off the beers by now and it was getting dark, so she lit some mosquito candles. I asked for some ice and shook up the cocktails. Holly was impressed I'd brought martini glasses, and loved the taste of the espresso martinis. She said she had no idea they were so simple to make, and would make them herself from now on. We actually had two each.

She thanked me for a lovely evening but said she had to turn in. I thanked her for the invite and staggered home. I actually thought it had been a *perfect* evening.

Of course, Jake got wind of my visit to Holly, and of course he asked did she have a boyfriend and did I think she would want to have a drink with him? I just said no to both.

He shrugged, 'Oh well, her loss.'

When I came out of the toilets, most of my colleagues had already gone.

Those that were still there asked was I OK? Said, 'It's a shock, isn't it?' I just nodded.

They were talking about having a coffee, even a drink although it was only about 11.00 am. I declined, and found myself just walking alone along the city streets, my mind spinning. I saw a bench in a small park and sat down in the shade under a huge tree, I felt very strange. Maybe because of my lack of sleep, the objects and trees around me seemed to have a sort of aura around them.

I was in a state of shock and disbelief. Also denial. Mark couldn't be dead! But if he was, could my wild thoughts actually be true? What I was thinking didn't seem possible. It was like a movie or TV show, it couldn't be real life.

Last night had been bad enough. But today was just surreal, unknown. While I was still sitting there, nothing was actually certain yet.

But I knew. I was sure.

I also knew what I had to do, now, before I got too scared. If I was wrong, fantastic. Worst case scenario was that I might be laughed at, ridiculed, maybe even charged with wasting police time. But if I was right, I needed to be safe. I had to trust that the police and the law would work the way they were supposed to. I wasn't absolutely certain that that would be the case though, I wasn't certain of anything. And if I was wrong, how would Z react?

The longer I sat there, the harder it became to move. I don't know how long I stayed there, frozen. I was startled when a young man pushing a pram entered the park. He stopped under another shady tree and laid a tartan picnic blanket out on the grass. Next were a couple of baby toys, and then he lifted his toddler out of the pram. The toddler managed a few steps on the blanket, then sat down and chuckled. It was a charming scene, life moving forward.

I forced myself to stand up and start walking. I don't know how long it took, time seemed to slow right down. It seemed like I wasn't getting any closer to my destination, then all of a sudden, I was there.

I stood still for about a minute just gazing up at the large glass and steel building in Spencer Street. The main city police station was fairly new, I'd never been inside, never had any reason to go there. I knew my life was going to change forever. I hoped it would be a good change for me, I thought it would. Taking a deep breath, I climbed the steps and pushed open the heavy door.

Inside was a bit confusing, but I found the front desk, and queued up, one other person was ahead of me. It was an elderly woman, I think she was getting directions. Then it was my turn. The officer on duty was a young female in uniform with hard eyes. I was so nervous, swallowed a few times and then managed to get some words out.

'I've got some information about the murder today.'

She looked stunned, probably expecting something more minor. She blinked, then spoke to someone on the phone. A young male in uniform came out, showed me to a room and asked me to wait. I was sort of expecting a mirror on one wall, but there was just a desk with a computer, a chair on each side and solid grey walls.

It seemed a long wait, but was probably only about ten minutes. A middle aged man in plain clothes came in. He looked strong, tough, was bald and a little bit overweight. He had kind eyes.

He introduced himself as Mick, and asked what had brought me there today. I took a deep breath and started speaking.

Mick listened carefully, took me seriously, asked some questions, set things in motion. I made a formal statement.

Mick later told me that when police officers went to our flat, Z was shocked to see them. He denied everything, demanded to see me, said I was delusional.

The only problem was Z's clothes were covered in blood and Mark's DNA.

The police worked out that Z had gone very early into the city and waited by the car park under the building I worked in. He had just followed the first car in, which he knew would be Mark. Then he had attacked Mark from behind as soon as he got out of the car, with a thick branch he had picked up from a park.

Mark would have been completely taken by surprise, unable to defend himself. He wouldn't have even known why he was being attacked.

When Mark was dead, Z had just dropped the branch, walked out of the car park and walked home. He had been wearing black clothes on purpose so the blood was hidden and he didn't attract any attention.

I had walked into the city a different way, or we might have met up. Z had taken short cuts through laneways, he would have gotten back home not long after I'd left. He would have been livid that I wasn't there. He'd tried to call me, had filled my message bank in fact. These were the messages he left:

'Where are you? You need to come home right now, I'm really sick and need your help.

'I'm so sorry about last night, I was wrong, don't worry about anything, just come home now, I really need you.

'I feel so bad, I've taken some sleeping pills and I might take more if you don't come home.'

Then his tone changed:

'You really need to come home right now if you don't want things to get worse for you.

'Where the fuck are you? How dare you ignore my messages. Believe me, it'll be better for you if you come home RIGHT NOW!'

I was incredibly lucky that I'd forgotten my phone that day. Because if I'd had it with me, and didn't know about Mark, I would have gone home.

And I'm absolutely sure Z would have killed me too, and then maybe himself. Or maybe not himself. But he didn't seem to care about the CCTV in the carpark, made no attempt to hide his face. Why didn't he kill me first? I'm not sure. Maybe Z wanted the pleasure of telling me what he had done, and that it was my fault. He wanted to enjoy my reaction, my fear. I try really hard not to think about what he would have done next.

Anyway, maybe those gods I don't believe in *had* been watching over me?

Z changed his story many times, and went through a few different lawyers. He had never trusted lawyers, thought they were all in cahoots.

At the trial, I gave my evidence clearly, without emotion, and without looking at Z.

The DNA evidence was solid.

I think Z chose the wrong lawyer, the one he engaged seemed to lack experience. The lawyer allowed Z to go into the witness box and speak for himself. It was a huge mistake. Z contradicted himself, denied, ranted, went off on tangents about betrayal, his lawyer couldn't control him at all. The judge actually had to tell Z to stop speaking.

The jury took less than a day to find Z guilty of first degree murder, and he was sentenced to 25 years, eligible for parole in 20.

I was tremendously relieved, I almost felt reborn. 20 years of freedom and safety lay ahead of me.

As Z was being led away, he turned to look at me and said very deliberately and loudly, 'When I get out, I'm going to find you and kill you.' He just stated it as a cold hard fact. I knew, and he knew I knew, that he meant it.

End of August 2022

I've just got home from a disastrous "date" with Jake. He hates me now, which is not a good thing.

I always knew he was interested in me, by the way he looked at me, and hung around me. I was very careful not to give him any encouragement. But he saw encouragement where none was given.

He would appear magically when I got back from my walk, and chat about the weather. He wasn't just being friendly, he'd been inviting me for a drink now and then, I'd always found an excuse like I was too tired or needed to finish a chapter. Or I just said no thanks with a smile. I thought of saying I didn't drink, but he knew I did because he'd seen me having a cocktail or two on my veranda. I knocked him back so many times I thought he surely would have taken the hint and given up, but he didn't. He persisted. It's like beggars or charity collectors, they put you in the position where you have to be rude to them to get rid of them, and I didn't quite want to do that. I didn't want to make an enemy in such a small town.

I suppose Jake was attractive in a puppy dog sort of way, but I was not at all interested. I also thought he seemed lonely and a bit aimless, but that was not my problem.

Anyway, today when I got back from my walk, he waylaid me. He told me it was his birthday, and invited me to have a drink at the club, said he wouldn't take no for an answer. He added that his Mum would be there and maybe a few other people that I would know. I thought he must mean Fran and maybe Sam, who are really the only people I know here. I thought well, if they are going, why not, it might be fun and just maybe I was a bit lonely too. So I said OK, but I still didn't have ID to sign in at the club.

He was surprised and pleased and said, 'Don't worry about signing in, I'll fix that. Great! I'll pick you up at 7 o'clock.'

I wondered if I'd done something stupid, but it was too late now. And I actually did want to go to the club, see what it was like inside. I decided what the hell, and put on my reversible dress and good shoes for the first time, I was glad I was actually going to use them.

Jake knocked on my door at 7.00 pm on the dot and handed me a bunch of flowers. They were drooping a bit and he'd left on the price tag from the petrol station. I was mortified.

He said, 'You look nice!'

All I could say was thanks. He was wearing clean jeans and a striped shirt, which was quite different to his usual shorts and t-shirt, and had slicked his hair back (usually it hung in his eyes).

We made awkward small talk as we walked to the club. I asked, 'Who else is coming?'

'Actually, they couldn't make it, it's just us.'

I should have known. I considered bailing but couldn't come up with a good enough reason. And hey, maybe I should give him a chance. But I also thought, how dare you.

At the club, he introduced me to the woman behind the counter, stating, 'This is my Mum, Sharon!' Sharon looked a bit older than me, lots of makeup on sun damaged skin, pale tired looking hair. She smiled at me in a slightly suspicious way, I didn't feel a lot of warmth coming my way from her.

She said, 'So you're the writer? Romance novels? I've read lots of them, would I have read one of yours?'

'No, it's my first one.'

'Well good luck, hope I can read it one day. Just put your ID in the machine here, please'

Jake jumped in, 'I told you, she doesn't have ID, it got stolen!'

She frowned, 'But the club could get fined.'

'Who's gonna know?' he demanded.

She sighed and let us in.

The club was quite flash inside, different areas, gaming, cafe, function rooms etc. Lots of money from the gambling for upkeep, I suppose. Jake talked me into having a meal, he said the food was really good here and I thought, okay, why not give it a try seeing I'm here.

He led me to the restaurant section and importantly asked the elderly waitress for a table for two. I could see him looking around to see if there was anyone there he knew, but it seemed there wasn't. We were shown to a table at the window which was good because I didn't have to keep looking at him. The restaurant was curved, and included an impressive looking pizza oven. The view was of an outdoor area with an island bar, and tables under umbrellas. A hunger-making smell of cheese and garlic was in the air.

We had to go and buy our drinks from the outside bar. Jake wanted to buy mine, but I bought my own Aperol Spritz, and he chose a beer. We both ordered pizza.

Conversation was awkward, I kept having to deflect his questions, so I asked him about himself instead.

'Well, I'm an only child and I live with Mum just down the road.'

'What about your dad?'

'Never met him. Arsehole left before I was even born!'

I asked, 'Did you ever try and find him?'

'Nah, not interested.'

He continued his life story. 'I left school as soon as I could. Hated it, waste of time! But then, I couldn't get a job. All me friends moved away, for work or Uni, I'm the only one left in Tomakin. I was happy enough just surfing, skating, playing games on me phone. But then Mum got me the job at the cabin park, cos she knows Fran. It's alright, I 'spose, the money's good. I did like the gardening, but that's finished now.'

'Would you like to do gardening as a job?'

'Dunno. Maybe. What I *wanna* do is go to Sydney, never been there.'

'What would you do in Sydney?' I asked.

'Just look round, I guess.'

There was a pause. Jake had finished his beer quickly and joined the queue to get another one. I was only halfway through my spritz, I was trying to make it last.

While he was queueing, I listened discretely to the two women at the next table. They didn't look like locals, being a bit too well dressed. One woman was blond, had a slim face and was wearing fashionable flared jeans. The other one had dark hair and a slightly rounder face, she was wearing fashionable torn jeans and high boots. The women seemed about my age and looked a bit similar, maybe they were sisters? I didn't think they would be staying at the caravan park, they seemed more the Airbnb type.

The "sisters" were a few drinks in by now, the blond one said something, the dark one disagreed and the blond one retorted bluntly, 'You're wrong, it's not like that at all! It's like this.' And then they just moved on and started talking about another subject. It was actually brilliant. There was no escalation, no argument, no raised voices, no insults. I was really impressed. I thought they should teach that technique in schools, a non-harmful way to disagree with someone.

Z could never let anything go in an argument. He not only had to win, but I had to say I was wrong.

Jake came back and we finished our meal and continued our uneasy conversation. I felt like I needed another drink, so I bought another spritz, Jake was pleased and got his third beer.

I'm sure he was trying his best, but I just didn't warm to him. There was nothing there, no opinions, no interest in the outside world, and I didn't like the way he called Fran "the old dragon."
I asked him about Sam, thinking he would know/like him. I was brought back to reality with a bang.

'The old Chink? He's been around forever, doesn't talk to anyone.'

'He's actually Vietnamese,'

'Same thing. When I was a kid, a bunch of us would go and throw rubbish in his boat.'

'Why?'

He shrugged, 'Just something to do.'

There was an uncomfortable silence.

Jake cleared his throat and said, 'You know, I think you're beautiful.'

I snorted out my drink. When I could, I asked, 'How old are you, Jake?'

'25.'

'And how old is your Mum?'

'42.'

I said, 'Well, I'm 45.'

He looked a bit shocked, but recovered well and said, 'Well you don't look it, you look like you're in your 30s!'

He was waiting for me to be flattered, but it didn't happen.

He went on, 'Anyway, I think you're interesting and different and I wanna get to know you better. What I'm trying to say is, would you like to be my girlfriend?'

I took a deep breath and thought, how dare you put me into the position of having to hurt your feelings.

While I was choosing my words, he actually added, 'It'd be good for your image to have a younger boyfriend, don't you think?'

I thought, really? You think THAT will win me over? It was an easy decision for me, clinched by his racism.

I didn't hold back. 'Sorry, but I'm not remotely interested in being your girlfriend. You seem like a nice guy,' I lied, 'But we've got nothing in common and I'm not at all attracted to you. If you want sex, you should just go somewhere and pay for it.'

'I don't want sex (well I do) but it's just that I've never had a girlfriend, I'm lonely and anyway, there's no one else around!'

I stood up and said, 'I'm going now. And just to be clear, I'd never, ever be your girlfriend. So stop hanging around me. OK?' He nodded with a red face.

So that was the end of the night. He didn't walk me home.

2008 ONWARDS

Once Z was securely locked up, the world completely changed for me. I felt like I existed again, like I could breathe. But, I knew he was still out there somewhere and was thinking about me. It was like a big invisible rock was hanging over me, waiting to crush me one day in the future.

Most people are lucky enough to go through life with no knowledge of how twisted some people can be. Anyone can be a killer, Agatha Christie wrote, if the situation is right. She also thought that some people are born evil. I agree with that.

Mick contacted me now and then and kept me updated about Z's time in prison. Mick had a contact in the jail, and apparently Z had "found God," was helping the chaplain, had become a model prisoner. Mick was sceptical. I was sure it was all a con, I knew how devious Z was, how he could exploit people's good nature. And even if he had found redemption, so fucking what?

I moved on with my life as best I could, lived alone, which I found suited me really well. Over the years I became quite happy with my own company. I read a lot and watched movies. I think you are never lonely if you have a good book, and a good movie will make the real world disappear for a while. For me, a good book is one I don't want to put down, one I lay awake reading long after I should be asleep. A good movie for me is one that makes me laugh and makes me cry. In the same movie.

I found an apartment I really liked, in Port Melbourne. It was up high, had a view of the ocean, I loved living there. I could swim in the sea, walk along the beach and walk into town which only took an hour.

Now and then I went on a few dates, mainly just because of loneliness, but I was definitely *not* looking for a relationship. I was too scarred and/or scared.

But then I met Paul, when I was in my late thirties. We first came across each other at a work function, he was in a different department, we just somehow clicked. Paul was a refreshingly nice guy, they actually *do* exist. He was mild mannered, quiet, I was the boss. He was also a few years younger than me.

We took it very slowly, it started as friendship and then developed. And then I got pregnant. Completely unplanned and out of the blue. I had actually thought I was too old. But the pregnancy test was positive and the blood test confirmed it.

Paul was taken aback at first, but then seemed happy. I was ecstatic. I thought he would be a wonderful dad, kind and gentle. We immediately made plans to move in together as soon as possible. I found it all a bit hard to believe to be honest, after all this time. Physically, I felt great, when I looked in the mirror I looked good, I could see that "glow" they talk about. We picked out baby names, planned marriage down the track. I had never felt so happy. And this was very likely my last and only chance to have a baby.

Then one day, after about ten weeks, I started bleeding a bit. I was at work, I couldn't believe it was happening to me. But when I looked in the mirror, the glow seemed to be gone. Still, I hoped I was wrong, that it was just something minor. I told work, they sent me to a busy medical centre nearby. The harassed looking receptionist told me it would be a long wait, I told her I was pregnant and had started bleeding. She actually looked annoyed then, but arranged for a doctor to see me straight away. The doctor thought I was probably OK, but put me in a taxi to hospital just to check. I got through to Paul, he sounded shocked and promised he would come as soon as he could.

At the hospital, I had to sit in a room with other women waiting to have their procedures. Two women were there for IVF, and they were chatting. One of them asked the young woman next to her if she was having IVF too. The young woman said no, she was there for an abortion, her boyfriend was married and didn't want her to have the baby. The first woman apologised, said she didn't mean to pry. There was silence after that.

After about half an hour, my name was called. I had to change into hospital garments, I was trying not to worry but that was impossible. An older nurse with a kind face came and led me to the ultrasound department. She squeezed my hand and told me someone would be with me soon. I spent the time reading and rereading a poster on the wall which had the title, "SEEING WITH SOUND!" and explained how ultrasounds actually worked. This I found fascinating, and it kept my mind occupied.

The technician who saw me was young, brisk and efficient. As she was running the sticky instrument over my stomach I had to ask, 'Is everything alright?'

She replied, 'I can't find any life.' Just like that.

I was sent to a ward to wait to have a dilation and curettage procedure. I was told this often happened with first pregnancies, it just meant that something wasn't quite right, and it was better for it to happen fairly early. Lying there on the bed, I couldn't stop crying. An outreach person came. I asked if she could get me some tissues, she assured me she would come back with some, but she never did.

I thought to myself, how tough do I have to be? I had crazy thoughts that maybe the gods had decided no, not this time, we saved your life, now we take one back.

Paul finally arrived after I'd had the operation. I was still crying, he didn't say much, I don't think he knew what to say or how to handle my grief.

I took time off work, just stayed in bed, Paul stayed with me for the first few days. I didn't want to go anywhere or do anything. After a week or so, Paul told me I needed to get out of bed, he had lost a child too but life goes on.

I felt like I didn't know him any more, he didn't show me much sympathy, he was like a stranger. I started talking to a grief counsellor, which did help me, and he started bonking his secretary.

What great therapy this writing has proved to be. I have just realised, as I am writing this, that even though it ended badly with Paul, that relationship was nothing at all like my relationship with Z. What happened with Z was not caused by me in any way. I didn't choose or attract the wrong type of guy, I didn't invite his behaviour or somehow bring it upon myself, and it didn't change because of something about me. Maybe I did ignore warning signs, but they were only visible in hindsight. What happened to me could happen to anyone. And you won't know until it's too late.

With Paul, even though I didn't understand his behaviour at the end, I still thought he was a decent enough person overall, and I always felt emotionally safe with him.

So then, I finally realised that I am truly better off on my own. I settled back into being single, joined a few groups to get out of the house (book, movie, walking), travelled overseas a bit by myself. I even did a creative writing course, but didn't actually go ahead and do any writing.

Every six months or so, Mick or someone else from the police rang me just to check in, which I appreciated.

Early on I had thought of changing cities, but I loved living in Melbourne. I knew I would have to already be gone, far away, when Z got out though. So I built up my escape fund and made my plans. I never got any pets I would have to leave, for example. And after Paul, there were no more relationships. My choice. So here we are now, up to date.

PART 3

After the "date," for the next few days Jake kept giving me dirty looks, or pointedly avoided me. I was actually quite pleased about that. It turned out to be more comfortable for both of us if we just stayed out of each other's way. Then he started giving me strange looks, more calculating ones, which I ignored.

It was late afternoon, a cool, cloudy day. I'd been for my walk, had stopped in at the café for a coffee, and entered the cabin park via the front gate.

Fran was walking awkwardly along the path, struggling a bit to carry a tin of paint. I asked her where Jake was, realising I hadn't seen him for a few days.

'Oh, he's gone, quit. Come into some money, he said. He's gone to Sydney.'

The air seemed to become charged, like before a storm.

I asked casually, 'Really? Where'd he get the money from?'

She replied that he didn't say. Then she asked, 'Are you alright? You've gone pale.'

'Yeah, I just need to do something. See you later!'

I rushed down to the beach, and walked as quickly as I could along the sand, saying, 'No, no, no!' to myself.

After about ten minutes, I spotted the elephant-shaped rock in the bush, then turned inland and walked quickly along the winding bush track. Everything looked the same as usual.

I counted the gum trees along the left hand side, until I got to the tenth one. Its base *seemed* to be undisturbed. Crouching, I dug down into the soft brown sandy earth with my hands. My little plastic box was still there, as was the money in it.

Relieved, I sat down. Maybe Jake *had* come into some money after all, from family, or maybe he'd had a win at the club? But still, something felt wrong, and he *had* been giving me those strange looks. I made a split second decision, took out all the money and tucked it into my bag. I was still spooked. I felt danger in the air, it was time to go.

I should have followed my instincts and just taken off with the cash. Gone straight to the bus stop, got on the next bus and got the hell out of Dodge. But I just wanted to get my stuff, and say goodbye to Fran.

I would miss my quiet life at the cabin park, and talking to Fran and Sam, but there was the rest of Australia to choose from. Maybe I'd find somewhere even better. Still, I was full of regret that I would have to leave Tomakin, this warm blanket of a place.

I hurried back to the cabin park, entering via the beach path. I could see Reception was now closed, but the lights were on inside. I paused and looked around carefully. Everything seemed the same as usual; it was quiet, no one was about. Walking quickly up to my cabin, my hands were a bit shaky and I dropped my key. I picked it up, and as I was unlocking my door, I was pushed suddenly from behind and stumbled forwards into the cabin.

I just managed to keep my footing and spun around. It was Z. He was standing there, with a smile that didn't reach his eyes. Shutting the door, he locked it, then stood with his back to it, solidly, arms folded.

'Sit down!' he ordered quietly.

I ran to the kitchen and managed to wrench open the kitchen drawer where the knives were. But he was faster, easily grabbing my arms from behind. I did my best to fight but he was so much stronger, pinning my arms back easily. He pulled cable ties out of his pocket and secured my wrists together behind my back, then threw me roughly face down onto the sofa.

I struggled, managing to sit up. I thought about screaming for help, but my cabin was too far from Reception to be heard.

Z kept standing, towering over me, his pale eyes boring into me. I wriggled on the sofa, as away from him as I could get. He commented, 'You look good. Older, but still attractive. So it *was* you that day, I thought it was.'

I said nothing, it was all I could do. Catching my breath, I felt strangely calm. In a way, almost relieved. I had always known this day was coming. Now it was right here, right now. No more waiting.

Z teased, 'Don't you want to know how I found you?'

The silence dragged on.

He continued, 'I knew you didn't get on the flight to Tasmania, but that phone thing was clever. I kept looking for you at the airport and then it seemed like you'd moved to a landfill site in Tullamarine, haha! But I was *always* going to find you. And you've made it easy for me, no-one knows who you are.'

He lost his calm and started raving; how I'd broken his heart, how he still loved me even though I'd betrayed him, why wasn't he enough for me? How he couldn't sleep, I was always in his thoughts, and when he did sleep, I was in his dreams. He said that he had a good chance for a new life now, but while I still existed, he couldn't move on.

I knew he was waiting for me to show fear, cry, plead maybe. What I did instead was yawn and remark, 'You mean nothing to me. You never did. You're just a sad, pathetic loser. My life is *so* much better now, without you.'

He smiled, 'Well, now there'll be *no* life for you.'

When he put his hands around my throat, I managed to spit in his face. I was pleased about that.

The pressure increased, and I lost consciousness.

31 August 2022

Gradually, I became aware of my surroundings. I was lying on my back on my sofa, Fran was calling my name urgently. A look of relief spread across her face when I opened my eyes. My throat was *really* sore.

Fran gently helped me sit up. 'I'll get you some water and cut these ties off.'

I saw that Z was lying on the floor on his back, his wrists joined together in front with cable ties. His ankles were also joined. He was out cold, a wound in his knee pulsing dark blood into a slowly spreading pool on the lino.

I was glad Fran had secured the danger first, in so many movies someone doesn't do that and the injured person gets back up and attacks again. Even though Z was tied up and unconscious right now, I could feel the danger of him.

There was a strange, burnt smell in the air. I noticed a rifle was propped up in the corner of the room. And there was the metallic smell of blood, like in a butchers shop.

I also noted that there had been no attempt to bandage Z's wound.

Fran cut off my cable ties with some scissors from the kitchen, and I rubbed my wrists. She brought me a glass of water which I coughed up at first. I managed to get some down, and it did make me feel a bit better. I was in a state of utter disbelief. That I was still alive, for one thing.

I croaked, 'Did you *shoot* him?'

'Yes.'

'Did you call the police?'

'No. Not yet.' There was a moment of silence.

Then she told me that he had arrived about half an hour ago, and asked if I was staying there. He had described me and added that he wasn't sure what name I would be using. He claimed that he was my cousin who had been living in South America, and hadn't seen me for a long time. Now he was back in Australia for a brief visit and had decided to look me up. He said he'd got a postcard of Tomakin from me a month ago, and wanted to surprise me.

'He seemed friendly, and harmless enough. But I didn't believe him, I had a gut feeling something was wrong. There were too many holes in his story. Why didn't he know the name you were using? And there *are* no postcards of Tomakin, at least none that *I* know of!

'So I told him you *had* been staying here but you'd left a week ago. And I didn't know where to, you hadn't said.

'I don't know if he believed me or not. He just shrugged and said, "Oh well, worth a try."

'He said he'd just stay the one night then, seeing he was here, and head off early in the morning. I suggested he go to the club for a drink and dinner. He said, 'Thanks for that! I will, after I've had a bit of a lie down.'

Fran decided to try and warn me, and keep an eye on him. She thought that if he *was* genuine, she would just apologise to us both and admit she'd got it wrong, but had just wanted to protect me.

Fran had watched him go into his cabin, then waited by her window.

She saw me coming up the path and came out warn me, but Z was too quick. She was shocked to see him rush out of his cabin and push me roughly through my door. So she went to get her gun.

'I didn't know you *had* a gun!'

'Well, it's my husband's. He used to shoot wild pigs. I just kept it in case I ever needed it.'

The gun was stored locked away in a cupboard in the gym. Fran grabbed it, then she had to remember where she kept the bullets. She did remember (in a box in the office), and then loaded the gun as quickly as she could. After grabbing the master key, she had listened briefly from outside my cabin, what she heard had made her unlock the door.

'He had his hands around your throat, you looked dead! I yelled at him to stop, he just looked up at me. Then he smiled! So I shot him. *That* wiped his smile off!

'I'd aimed at his legs and got him in the knee. He sort of spun round and fell heavily on his back, he must have hit his head and passed out. Some cable ties had fallen out of his pocket so I tied him up. And then I woke you.'

She asked, 'Who *is* he?'

I told her my story as quickly as possible. Even so, it took me a while. Staring down at him lying there, I tried to explain him, what he was like, how he thought. And then, what he had done and why he was here. Even to me it sounded unbelievable, like a B-grade movie plot.

Fran had listened in complete silence. Her expression was unreadable.

She commented, 'So that's why you're here. I didn't think you were a writer.'

And then she asked, 'What do you want to do now?'

'What do you mean?' I asked slowly.

She replied, 'Anything's possible.'

To this day, I don't truly understand what motivated her to help me.

For me, the solution was crystal clear. I knew, beyond a shadow of a doubt, that if Z went back to jail, he would just get out one day, and hunt me again. Maybe he would be locked up for good, but that never seems to happen.

But Fran had a choice. This was not her problem, at all. Why would she risk everything? All I can really think of is because of what happened to her in the past.

Of course I considered the possibility that someone would come looking for him. But somehow, I didn't think so. I did ask Fran if anyone would hear shots, she said maybe, but they'd just think it was someone pig shooting. And there'd already been one shot and no one had come to investigate. I asked, hopefully, if he would just keep losing blood and die? She said probably not, and pointed out that the blood had now stopped flowing.

I asked, finally, 'Are you absolutely sure about this?'

She didn't hesitate. 'Yes.'

So I made my decision.

I said, 'I don't want to run any more.'

1 September 2022, early morning

We were extremely lucky there was no moon that night. The stars provided just enough light to walk, although we did stumble a bit. Fran and I pushed the wheelie bin together, it was heavy and awkward, but manageable. Sam followed along behind, easily carrying the kettle bell.

We tried to be as quiet as possible, but the bin made quite a noise rumbling along the uneven planks of the pier. It was about 4.00 am by then, I think, silent as a grave except for the noise *we* were making.

Thankfully reaching the end of the pier, the three of us just stood there and caught up on our breathing. Then in mutual silence, working together, we awkwardly managed to tip the contents of the bin out into the bottom of Sam's boat. It fell with a sickening thud.

Fran said to me, 'I'll take the bin back, you go with Sam, unless you want to do the cleaning up? Didn't think so.'

Sam already had the engine running, I clumsily cast off and jumped in. He had lit a dim lantern at the front of the boat, just revealing the way about a metre forward. I stared straight ahead, carefully avoiding looking down into the boat. We sat in silence.

The lights on the shore blinked and became fainter. After about half an hour, there were no lights visible at all any more, we were surrounded by ocean. The waves were a fair bit rougher now and there was a cold breeze which made me shiver.

Sam switched off the engine. There was faint light now, beginnings of the sunrise, enough to see by. Sam worked quickly and efficiently, wrapping the body in a sturdy net. He tied a thick rope securely around it using some impressive knots. Finally, he attached the kettle bell to the rope with a chain.

He said, 'You help me now.'

Between us we managed to lift the awkward shape and manoeuver it over the side, the kettle bell pulled it straight down. There was a trail of bubbles and then nothing.

Sam took off his hat and I saw that he was quite bald. He stood and looked at the spot for a full minute. Then he turned to me and said, 'OK, we'll go back now.'

The trip back was again silent, the rising sun slowly turning the sky orangey pink and then blue. I felt something strange. I was a bit dizzy and lightheaded from lack of sleep, but I was shocked when I recognised the feeling I had. It was hope. I was shocked because I realised that I had not had this feeling for about twenty years.

It seemed to take less time going back, soon enough we pulled up at the pier. It was still early and there was no one around. Sam whispered, 'OK, no one's here, you go.'

I gave him a hug he wasn't expecting and whispered, 'Thank you.'

He just replied, 'Go quickly!'

The sun was getting stronger as I walked quickly along the pier, the temperature already in the 20s, it was going to be a glorious day. A mother and her young child were sitting on the beach in the distance, up early building a sandcastle. I watched them for a moment, and realised tears were running down my face.

When I unlocked my cabin door, Fran was asleep on my sofa. She woke with a start. There was a strong smell of bleach now, plus the lavender smell of the scented candle which was still burning but very low, almost out. Fran's Persian rug was now on the floor.

I wailed, 'Oh no, your lovely rug!'

She laughed grimly, 'I hate this rug. My husband bought it because *he* thought it looked classy, but *I* was the one who had to clean it.'

She asked, 'How did you go?'

'Fine, no problems.' I added, curiously, 'How did you know Sam would help?'

She just smiled and replied, 'He owes me.' I was curious, but didn't think now was the time to ask. She asked how I felt.

'Tired, numb. But lighter.'

She nodded. She said, 'Come with me,' and led me to her place. She told me to have a shower and then get some sleep in her bed. I was too tired to argue.

I made the shower as hot as possible, then climbed into her bed wrapped in a towel. I thought I wouldn't be able to get to sleep, but she sat with me like a mother until I dropped off.

Waking a few hours later, at first I wasn't sure where I was. Fran's bedroom was larger than mine, the walls were painted a duck egg blue. In the corner of the room sat a large, comfortable looking armchair, on it some clean clothes of mine had been laid out. I dressed quickly and joined Fran out in Reception.

She smiled and made me coffee, but I couldn't eat anything.

'How's your throat? she asked.

'Getting better.'

'And how's your shoulder?'

'A bit sore'

She grinned, 'I did warn you.'

Then she said, 'You have to go.'

I nodded, 'I know.'

We walked to my cabin. She had packed all of my stuff into my suitcase, but hadn't found my cards. I'd hidden them in the Bible, because I was pretty sure no one would ever look there. I showed them to her, she exclaimed, 'So that's your name!'

I looked around my "home" for the last time with a feeling of deep regret, then started wheeling my suitcase out to the carpark.

Fran told me to hang on a minute, and walked back into her place. She emerged a minute later carrying some rubber gloves and a small brightly patterned silk scarf. She tied the scarf loosely around my neck to hide the bruises which she insisted looked shocking. When she had it tied to her satisfaction, she actually laughed and told me I looked like a flight attendant. I laughed too but that made me cough.

Pulling on the gloves, I unlocked the boot of Z's car and lifted my suitcase in.

I tried to give Fran my remaining cash but she wouldn't hear of it, insisted she didn't need it.

'Well what about Sam?'

She thought for a moment. 'Maybe.'

I took out enough for my next few days and she promised to give him the rest. We hugged for a long time.

I said, 'Anything. Anything you need. Any time.'

She just nodded, we both had tears. I fitted on my trusty black wig and drove off.

1 September 2022

As I drove past the club, I saw a huge sign stating "Nick and Marta's 70th Wedding Anniversary This Saturday!" I wondered if it was the same Nick that got off the bus when I arrived. 70 years, how utterly amazing!

The drive to Sydney took about four or five hours. Luckily the car was three quarters full of petrol and I didn't have to stop, except for a quick break at a roadside toilet block. The car was comfortable to drive, a red Suzuki Swift with Victorian plates. I assumed it was a rental car, it was not really the sort of car Z would buy. When I was with him, he'd had a Ford Falcon.

Z's phone, which was in my bag, made noises now and then. I ignored it. If someone was trying to contact him, I didn't want to know about it. My throat was still very sore, it was hard to swallow, but that gradually eased as time went on. It was a bizarre feeling driving in rubber gloves, my hands got quite sweaty.

I became totally lost in Sydney, drove around the narrow busy streets for ages until I finally spotted signs for Circular Quay. Thankfully, I parked the car in a quiet, narrow side street near an old factory. I left the car unlocked, and the keys on the seat. Retrieving my suitcase from the boot, I walked off quickly.

Soon I reached Circular Quay. The first thing I did was drop the gloves into a bin. I stored my suitcase in a locker, then bought a ticket on the next ferry, which happened to be going to Manly. It was only about a five minute wait until the ferry left, not many people taking the journey in the middle of the day. Passengers on board were a large family group of Asian tourists with kids, a handful of tradies, two tall blond European guys with large backpacks.

The green and yellow older style ferry had two levels, and was named "Charlotte." All the passengers including me climbed up and sat on the top level, enjoying the sights. I listened to the backpackers talking about how they were blown away by Sydney, and were planning on going on a long coastal walk the next day, from Bondi to Coogee.

Sydney harbour was a spectacular sight, the water bright blue and sparkly. After a reasonable time, I climbed back down to the lower level and stood at the side of the ferry. No one else was there. I pretended I saw something in the water, leaned over to have a look and casually dropped Z's phone into the water. The ferry was going at a fair pace, and the phone disappeared quickly from sight. I felt elated, this was the last thing I had to do.

My plan had been to stay on the ferry and go straight back, but I thought, why not have a look at Manly? I'd never actually been there. So I climbed down off the ferry behind the tourists. Not far from the pier was an intriguing pavilion that had a Middle Eastern look. It had a restaurant right on the water, but was *way* too expensive for me, so I walked through the mall and had lunch at a corner pub on the other side. It had an attractive, sheltered rooftop with a view. I chose oysters and a prosecco, in fact two, to celebrate. A feeling of freedom and yes, happiness washed over me and I started to cry, which got some curious looks from a nearby table of blokes in suits.

The ferry was more crowded on the way back, and the water was rougher, so I didn't enjoy the trip as much. I was also feeling really tired, I actually nodded off now and then. Back on land I took my wig off in some toilets, retrieved my bag, and walked around until I found a hotel not that far away. A bit more upmarket than the last place I stayed, and pleasingly with an actual coffee machine in the room. They were happy to take cash too which surprised me, but maybe this area has more rich foreign tourists that prefer to pay that way.

Sydney seemed somehow easier to manage and friendlier this time round, but maybe that's just me. Tiredness hit me like a brick, I didn't even take my shoes off, just fell into the bed fully dressed.

I woke myself up by saying the words, 'It's over.' I just lay there and let that sink in. I'd slept for nearly 12 hours.

After a strongly-pressured shower, which felt truly amazing, I found the included breakfast on Level 1. It consisted of toast you made yourself, salad and barista coffee.

Reception gave me directions to the City of Sydney Library. It was another sunny day and a pleasant walk, partly through a large green park. I liked the fancy fountain there with turtles spraying water. The library was, as expected, a huge old sandstone building. At first I couldn't find the entrance but did find a cute statue of Matthew Flinder's cat, Trim, sitting on a roof. The main entrance was around the corner and had huge metal doors carved with images of sailing ships and indigenous people.

A helpful librarian directed me to computers where I could access the internet. I read through all the news sites, looking for stories of people reported missing, people released from jail, etc. There was nothing. Nothing at all. I hadn't really expected anything, after only one day, but it didn't hurt to check. After deleting my search history I left.

The rest of my day was spent walking around the harbour being a tourist. I found and sat in Mrs Macquarie's chair.

Tomorrow I'll try and get a ticket on the XPT back to Melbourne. It's time to go home.

2 September 2022

There was no ticket available for today's train, so I am going tomorrow. This time I'm travelling during the day. I'll see more scenery and won't have to try and sleep. So I've got one more day in Sydney to kill.

I decided to try the Bondi to Coogee walk, and it was truly fantastic. The day was perfect, mid 20s, ideal September weather for a long walk. I wore shorts and carried water.

I found (with difficulty) where to catch the bus to Bondi, but after that, it was all easy. Bondi itself has yellow sand and a couple of pools right above the ocean. There were interesting rock formations, and a pod of dolphins quite close to the shore, just hanging around. Dolphins are good for your soul.

The walk goes past lots of older style apartment buildings with balconies, and some grand newer houses with lots of glass. There are lots of steps, and each bay and inlet is completely different. One inlet just has concrete all the way around. There are rock pools, mosaic steps. At one point, the walk goes past a historic cemetery housing the remains of Henry Lawson.

I really, really enjoyed the walk, stopping for coffee and ice cream here and there. Being a weekday, there weren't loads of other people doing the walk, but there are always tourists. I imagine it would get really busy there on weekends with the locals as well.

Reaching Coogee at last, I climbed up to the top of the Pavilion for lunch. There was a really cool bar and restaurant up there. I sat outside of course, looking towards the ocean, and had a beer and a grazing platter with some interesting flavours. Then another beer.

I've *totally* changed my mind about Sydney. It's such a beautiful city, all these different little beaches and you *cannot* beat that harbour. It would be awesome actually living here, but that seems unaffordable unless you are rich. Although they do say Sydney is better to visit and Melbourne is better to live in. I think that's true.

Anyway, I'm glad my last day here has been so enjoyable. I splurged on a room service dinner and cocktail.

6 MONTHS LATER (ROUGHLY)

I'm sitting on my rented balcony, it's a balmy 32° at 6.00 pm, the ceiling fan above spins slowly. I'd never seen a ceiling fan on a balcony before but they are common here and necessary. My apartment is in a great spot, I can see the lagoon, the big ferris wheel, the ocean beyond. No-one actually swims in the ocean due to sharks, crocodiles and jelly fish but the lagoon is very popular. I often go down and splash around, to cope with the sweat and humidity. At first it was fabulous living here, I never felt cold, ever. The unofficial uniform is as little as possible and comfortable; just shorts, singlets and thongs. Or, even just a loose dress and thongs. Rent and food *are* expensive though, far more than they are back in Melbourne. The tyranny of distance.

Humidity here is otherworldly. I've been here before, on holidays, for a week or two. But that's *nothing* like actually living here. Sometimes I go through two bras per day because they get soaked through. I've had to buy shoes and sandals one size bigger, because my feet have swollen. I go for my walk early in the morning when it's coolest, but that's still in the high 20s. In the evening, it stays hot.

People drink a lot, mostly beer, I think mainly because it's bitter and that's what you want in the heat. Although rum is popular too.

But, I've actually stopped drinking every day. Now I only drink when I go out, or on a special occasion. I'd tried Feb Fast and Dry

July before, sometimes I failed and once the month was over, nothing changed. I'd also tried having one alcohol free day per week, but which day? Often that day didn't come. What I did this time, which seems to be working, is to drink non-alcoholic wine or beer at the same time of day I would normally have my first alcoholic drink, usually straight after I finish work. Not all non-alcoholic drinks are made equal, but I found brands that I *did* like the taste of. Then, after a few months, I found I didn't even need to do that anymore. I just had water, or juice instead. If I was out by myself and felt like a drink, I would choose one of the non-alcoholic versions and just have one. So I still *felt* like I was having a drink and didn't feel like I was missing out. Of course, if I was out with other people, I would have a real drink.

So now I feel healthier, younger and I am definitely sleeping better. And I can still drink if I really, really want to. Just not every day. Fingers crossed I can keep it up.

Cooling off in the water is the best way to cope with the heat, I find, and don't move unless you absolutely have to. Also good is sitting under a big tree, you get shade *and* air movement. And, of course, carry water and drink it all the time, don't wait for thirst. Always wear a hat, and walk slowly if you have to be out in the heat of the day. So those are my tips if you want to live up here. It's not for everyone, even if you think you like heat. I never really liked air conditioning before, I always thought it was too cold. Now, I love it. It's crucial.

When I got back to Melbourne, the first thing I did was buy a new phone. It folds in half, like my first ever red phone did, but this one folds in a different way. I love it but don't actually use it that much. My electricity had been disconnected, I'd forgotten *that* bill. Once I got it reconnected, I discovered that my coffee machine was leaking, a pipe had corroded, it was a tragedy. But, I ordered a new one and it was delivered three hours later, very impressive.

Apart from that, everything was fine. Lots of mail, mostly junk, had piled up. I had hundreds of emails, also mostly junk. There was loads of money in my bank account, my employer had paid me all my leave, even long service, I was stunned at the amount.

Melina was away on an extended overseas holiday, and *I* had been away so long that I felt like a stranger in my own home town. I stayed for a while, but every time I walked through the park to my street, I kept expecting to see Z there on the bench. So I walked along the street, but still had to go and check the bench every time, I couldn't stop myself. For the sake of my mental health, I felt the need to get right away, at least for a while. To go somewhere new and completely different.

So here I am in Darwin. First I tried Broome for a while, which was an amazing, unique place. I stood in dinosaur footprints and saw the rings of Saturn. But, it was extremely remote and just a bit too wild west for me. Darwin was next and I found it suited me better, it's big enough to feel like I'm in a city. But money was getting very low by then, so luckily I was able to get my job back. They'd actually kept it for me, had just put me on indefinite leave without pay. So now I'm now a "digital nomad" working remotely here on my balcony.

I do have a stove now, but I eat out most of the time. It's just too hot to feel like cooking, and there is good cheap Asian food everywhere which suits this climate. Money is not an issue now I'm working again, and there are lots of choices, so I live on takeaway or snacky dinners.

I've found a decent coffee place too, it's tiny, run by a lovely Kiwi guy. He only does coffee and toasties, and I just have the coffee. He has a loyal customer base and I am one of them.

Darwin has a different, remote, holiday feel. I love the rainbow steps and there is some magnificent street art. The buses can be a bit dodgy though.

People are generally friendly, and most of the ones I've met come from somewhere else. Mainly Adelaide, Brisbane, Perth and New Zealand. Not Sydney or Melbourne. Maybe people prefer to move somewhere bigger, not smaller?

It can get a bit wild and woolly in Darwin at night, but I mostly stay inside then, which suits me just fine. There will always be new Nordic Noir on SBS to get into.

I've finally joined Facebook, which is maybe not such a great thing, I really hate all the targeted ads, and the mindless scrolling I seem to be doing now. But it's an easy way to keep up with Melina's holiday. And I found my pen pal Chris Elwood! Her parents had died, that's why my letter was returned. We were both ecstatic to be in touch again. I gave her a brief outline of what had happened with Z, she was horrified. She seems happily enough married and has 2 kids. We write to each other on messenger about once a month now, and there are vague plans to meet in person one day. Maybe it might even happen.

Anyway, the reason I am writing here again after some time, is that I can now finish my story. I have the final piece of the puzzle. I got this email from Fran today:

"Hi, hope you are doing well wherever you are. This is my first ever email, the librarian in Batemans Bay showed me what to do! Things are just the same here. I've done some renovations, put new flooring in some of the cabins. Fake floorboards, much cooler and nicer to walk on than the lino. And I am charging more, people will pay! Win-win ☺

Jake came back about a month ago, had spent all his money in Sydney and wanted his old job back. I just said, sorry, can't afford to pay you, and I am managing just fine. He didn't believe me but there was nothing he could really do. He asked after you, I just said you'd gone, and I didn't know where to (which is true!) He also asked if anyone had come looking for you, which was a strange thing to ask, don't you think? I just said actually yes, but you'd already gone by then. I said why do you ask? He said, oh he'd just heard on the grapevine that someone was looking for you. I really wanted to ask, what grapevine is that? But I thought I'd better not. Anyway, he moped around for a few weeks and then told me he'd got a job at the Gold Coast, so he's gone, hopefully for good this time! Good riddance to bad rubbish, I say.

More recently, just yesterday in fact, the police came and asked about a guy who'd stayed here some months ago. I told them he'd just stayed one night, left early in the morning, was driving to Sydney, he said. I showed them the ledger and his room, they were satisfied and left. So that should be the end of that.

Sam says hi, he's put in a basic bathroom on his boat with some money he'd come into. So now he can have a shower out at sea! He says he is thinking of taking people out fishing, now that he has a bathroom, but I don't know if anything will come of that, I don't really think it would suit him. But you never know.

Anyway, I'm quite busy now, the season is in full swing, mostly Canberrans as usual, but quite a few from Sydney, and the odd ones from overseas. I'm seriously considering advertising on the internet, I reckon that would boost customers quite a bit, don't you think? I might even get a computer for the office, it's really not that hard, once someone shows me what to do. And I'm not stupid.

But enough about me, tell me about you, how you are going (if you want to of course). I'm sure you are doing just fine, and hope you have a great future.

It would be lovely to see you again one day if you want to drop in. Your cabin is the most popular one, being quiet, but it's yours whenever you want it, if it's free of course.

Anyway, best wishes and I hope your time here changed your life in a good way.

Love from your friend, Fran. Xxx"

A flood of emotion washed over me when I read that email. I felt immense gratitude and love towards her for what she did for me. It's the news I've been waiting for, and answers the question of how Z found me. Jake. When he was cleaning, he must have found my cards in the bible. Once he had my real name, he somehow found out who was looking for me. He's smarter than I thought. And much more ruthless.

So, now my story is finished, now that I know how Z found me. He almost didn't, but Jake was really my fault. I shouldn't have scorned him, OR let him find my cards. Young males with fragile egos, you never know what they are capable of.

On second thoughts, maybe it's not my fault at all. In any way. Maybe it's just bad luck.

That's really all I need to write. I can now, finally, think about the future. As Fran said, it's my choice. Do I stay here, at the hot top of Australia, do I go back to Melbourne, my cool tribe, the best coffee? Or do I go back to Tomakin, or maybe even Batemans Bay? I can work from anywhere now, even overseas. When I do settle, I can finally get a pet. A dog like Fugly, a cat like Luna, maybe even both?

And lastly, what do I do with this "book"? I don't want to burn it, although I should. But I've spent months writing it, it would be such a shame to destroy all these words. Haha, I know, I'll put it in a watertight container and set it adrift in the sea.

THE END

P.S.

There are some things I haven't put down on paper yet. To finish my story off properly, I really should write down everything that happened in my cabin in Tomakin on that last night.

So here goes.

Fran showed me what to do, but I did it. I'd never even touched a gun before, let alone fired one. I was scared at what it felt like, the power.

Emotionally, I felt nothing. Z became just a pile of flesh and bones, all his hatred and power were gone in an instant. As was my fear.

Then the night became like a parallel universe. I made us both Espresso Martinis, with shaking hands. We sat there drinking our cocktails and making our plans, a dead body at our feet.

The first thing we discussed and agreed on, was that calling the police and claiming self-defence wouldn't work. We quickly came to the unanimous conclusion that we had to make him disappear.

At that exact point, Z's phone rang and we both jumped. We just sat there looking at each other and waited until it stopped.

Fran had spilled her drink so I made her another one. Then, trying not to shudder, I managed to empty his pockets, which contained his phone, wallet and car keys. There was some cash in the wallet, but I put it back in his pocket, I didn't want to risk anything at all like serial numbers being traced etc. The phone and car keys I placed on my kitchen table, to be dealt with later. Fran wasn't sure about the phone, she thought it should stay with him but I explained to her how it could be tracked, and how that would be useful.

Next, she used her own phone to make her astonishing phone call to Sam. Luckily he wasn't far out at sea and promised he would arrive as soon as possible, probably about half an hour.

While we were waiting, Fran told me *her* story, which she had never told anyone else before, she admitted.

'I met Frank in New Zealand, we were both shearers.'

'Really? Wow!' I commented.

'He was an Aussie, very good looking! Swept me off my feet. I was *so* young and naïve.

'We got married, saved loads of money, and came to Australia. Frank had this dream of owning a caravan park, he thought it was an easy way to get rich. So we bought the land here, it was just a vacant block at the time. It took lots of hard, physical work to make it into a caravan park. And we lost a heap of money the first few years.'

It turned out that Fran's husband was both a gambler, and physically abusive to her. Frank treated her like a slave, told her that because she was a New Zealander, she had no rights in Australia. It wasn't true, but she didn't know that at the time.

Fran had no one in Australia to turn to, and was not close to her dysfunctional family back in New Zealand. Like with me, leaving seemed impossible. So she put up with it as best she could, wore long sleeves and scarves.

Finally, after years of hard work, they did start making good money, and things improved a bit. But Frank would often gamble large amounts at the club, and take it out on her if he lost. He never hit her face, just her body. His favourite place to punch her was her stomach, she thought that's why she never got pregnant.

One time he broke her arm, and was annoyed that *he* had to take her to the doctor. But she couldn't drive herself with a broken arm.

The doctor was in Bateman's Bay, he and his wife were friends of theirs, they would sometimes all go out for dinner or drinks as a group of four. At the doctor's surgery, they were told there might be a bit of a wait as the doctor was with another patient who had only just gone in. Frank decided to go and have a quick drink at the pub next door rather than sit in the waiting room. But the doctor was quick, so it turned out that Fran went in alone.

She took an enormous risk, and told the doctor that Frank had broken her arm. She could see he was shocked. He treated her arm in silence. Finally he said, 'Out of respect for our friendship Fran, I won't tell your husband what you said.'

Fran suffered at Frank's hands for years, and no one ever knew.

'I'm so sorry that happened to you!' I said.

She concluded, 'Then, one day there was an accident. He was cleaning his gun and it went off. He died of a gunshot wound to the head.'

Our eyes met.

At that exact moment, there was a loud knock on the door. This time, we *both* spilled our drinks. But it was Sam. Fran let him in, he surveyed the scene in silence. Then he asked some questions, had some ideas, like the wheelie bin.

I've already written about what happened next, but there a couple more things I want to say.

Never in my wildest dreams, did I imagine my story would end like this. That *I* would get rid of *him*. My hope was always just that I could successfully avoid him, forget him and live out my life in peace.

Firstly, I don't feel bad about what I did, I think it was absolutely necessary. He was in the process of trying to kill *me,* for God's sake! And also, he didn't know it was going to happen, unlike what he wanted to do to me. He had a good death.

Am I a monster, therefore? If I am, Z made me one. If I'd never met him, I think I would just be an ordinary person living a "normal" life, whatever that is.

I *do* feel bad about involving other people, but that was necessary too, and it was their choice. If I do somehow end up getting caught, I'll just say I stole Fran's gun, stole Sam's boat, did it all by myself.

But I'm not actually too worried about getting caught, I really feel like we've thought of everything. There is always some niggling worry, of course. But if I end up in jail, I'll cope. It would be worth it, for sure.

Sometimes I have vivid, petrifying dreams; that they find Z's bloated body floating in the ocean, sometimes I even see him fight his way out of the net and swim to the surface. But those dreams happen less and less as time goes on.

And finally, I've completely changed my worldview. There *are* some people you can trust.

ACKNOWLEDGEMENTS

First of all, thank you so much for taking the time to actually read my book. It means a lot to me. If you liked it, please spread the word, leave a review etc.

Thank you to Michelle K who said even if it doesn't get published, and no one ever reads it, you've actually gone ahead and written a book! Be proud of yourself.

Thank you to Suzanne for editing, and Liz for reading advice.

Thank you to my wonderful apartment neighbours Fiona, Penelope, Michelle R and Michelle S for their encouragement, and contacts.

Thank you Wal and Sam for gun advice.

Thank you KT for police advice.

Thank you Sonya for art advice.

Thank you to Laurie and Jayne for taking the trip with me.

And finally, thank you Tim and Chris, for being my family.

Tomakin is a real place. It has a café, a club and a caravan park. But no separate cabin park.

I have an idea for a second book, with some of the same characters from Not Tomahawk, set 20 years into the future. Stay tuned…

sites.google.com/view/sandydobson

www.ingramcontent.com/pod-product-compliance
Lightning Source LLC
Chambersburg PA
CBHW061156210726
48294CB00006B/1693